HIDDEN WORLDS
VOLUME 1

Jeffrey Peter Clarke

HIDDEN WORLDS
VOLUME 1

FICTION4ALL

Resurrection

No, Alessandro. No!'

Her hand gripped his wrist. Alessandro wavered, glanced aside at her then lowered the rifle.

'That officer,' he muttered angrily, 'he's SS. He's an important man. From here we could pick him off - and maybe the rest of those damned Nazis.'

'No, Alessandro,' sighed dark-eyed Carmella. She laid aside her own rifle, leaned against the crumbling stone wall, eyes turned to the sky above. Late afternoon sunlight filtered through the pine trees to cast a sheen on her long hair and a dappled pattern across her face. 'They're on the run. Where's the sense in risking our lives? There are eight of them and only two of us.'

Stern-eyed Alessandro peered over the wall, through the trees and across a road of rutted, hardened mud. The officer was shouting orders and two soldiers, bare-headed, begrimed and sweating in the heat, emerged from the ancient stone church carrying between them an ammunition box. This they heaved up into the rear of a drab green truck that had recently laboured its dusty way up from the direction of the village. Neither the soldiers nor their officer paid attention to the thud of a distant explosion, then another, that rolled on sultry air from the south. The explosions had been going on all day and for much of the day before.

'That bastard had four of our men shot,' growled Alessandro. 'It's unforgivable, you know. Unforgivable that we - that I, should not try to kill them all.'

'Look,' she breathed, placing a hand on his stubbled cheek,' the Americans are already in Florence and soon they will be here. Why risk our lives when others will do the job for us?'

'Why?' he answered, raising the gun once more, 'Because they say the Germans are preparing defences to the north. If they drive back the Americans and the British we'd be for it anyway.'

'No!' she insisted, seizing his arm as the rifle swung around. 'Our friends, our families - do you want them to suffer as well? And what about me, Alessandro? Yes, what about me?'

Alessandro looked into her eyes, propped his rifle by hers and leaned back against the wall. 'OK - have it your way. I suppose we've played our part.'

'That's right, Alessandro, we *have* played our part.'

Another explosion drifted up from the valley and as if in response, the truck engine spluttered into life. The officer was shouting again. Alessandro and Carmella peered through the trees to observe two soldiers heaving up what appeared to be boxes of files to those men already in the vehicle then scrambling up to join them. With protesting engine the truck rattled and lurched forward, swaying along the road, raising brown dust, coughing black smoke. Two more soldiers, muffled and goggled, weaved around from behind the church on chattering motorcycles. They steadied themselves then both raced ahead of the truck. The small convoy revved its way along the road to vanish from sight beyond the trees. Then silence.

Even the shellfire had abated though beyond the valley way to the south, a dark pall of ragged smoke hung against the blue haze. Alessandro regarded the smoke then reached into his shirt pocket to withdraw an all but ruined pack of cigarettes. They were aware now of birds singing.

'I suppose,' said Carmella, 'we should tell people in the village the Germans have left the church before we go back to our homes.'

'We can do that,' mumbled Alessandro, attempting to light a crumpled cigarette with his battered lighter. 'I'm not staying around the valley any longer than I can help. Whoever wins or loses, I'm going to join the Americans. They might need someone like me - an interpreter - someone who knows the area and speaks passable English. They'll have plenty of cigarettes, too. I hear the Americans always have cigarettes. You could come with me, Carmella. Yes, I think you should.'

'Me? If they'd take us on for good I'd jump at it. I'd like to go to America, Alessandro - wouldn't you? Everything is new there. New and clean and open. We have most of our lives ahead of us. We could have a fresh start and earn good money.'

'We might not see our friends and our families for a long time,' he said.

'You weren't so bothered about them a few minutes ago,' she responded.

'We can talk about it tonight,' he said thoughtfully, blowing out a stream of smoke as he gazed across the deserted road. 'I'd like to go as well. They say there's plenty of work and good money to be made. Yes, plenty of dollars. We could go together. Yes, we could get married and go to New York. Better than farming pigs and chickens in the valley. No more petty feuds, no more family

7

squabbles and no more turning spadefuls of shit. No more living in the past with ignorant peasants. What d'you say?'

'Oh, yes, I'd like that. Once this war is over - yes. A new life, Alessandro – all the things we could never have here. Everything new.'

'I'm going to take a look inside the church,' he muttered, throwing aside the remains of the cigarette. 'The Germans might have left something behind.'

'Left something?' she queried. 'They will have taken everything - you see. If there was anything valuable belonging to the church they will have taken that as well.'

'There was never much in that church from what I remember.'

'So you have been inside,' responded Carmella. 'I thought the people from your village never came here. I'm surprised it hasn't fallen into ruin.'

'We came here once when I was at school,' he replied as both picked up their rifles. 'It was some special occasion – maybe a saint's day. I don't remember what. Everyone used to say it was too far away even though they preferred it to our new church. The old village near here was abandoned well over a century ago. It's all overgrown and not easy to see from the road. Now the Germans are gone I can show you the ruins. Maybe tomorrow.'

'Why did the people move away?' asked Carmella.

'Why? I'm not sure why,' responded Alessandro, slinging the rifle over his shoulder. 'I heard all sorts of weird tales when I was at school. Something very bad happened and they were forced to go. None of the adults ever talked about it. You know how superstitious they are. I hate all that.'

The thud of two more detonations rolled dully by.

'Let's go,' said Carmella, shouldering her own gun. 'I want to see inside there as well.'

Still cautious, they stepped through the trees toward a gap in the wall. Alessandro gestured with his hand as they went. 'A stray shell landed hereabouts last night - I saw it from my village.'

'Oh, well at least it didn't hit the church.'

'Not the church, no, and not the damned Germans more's the pity, and I didn't see any damage on the road - but I saw the explosion.' Pointing to their right he added, 'Maybe it was over that way - near the cemetery.'

'I think so, too,' agreed Carmella. 'Look, there are branches hanging down over there by those old tombs.'

'I don't suppose the residents care about that now,' grinned Alessandro.

'As you say, what does it matter. We should think of the living rather than the dead. After the war is over I hope people will do that.'

'After the war is over,' began Alessandro, 'you and I will make a new start and -'

Carmella hesitated, her gaze fixed toward the damaged trees.

'What is it?' he asked.

'Alessandro - there is someone watching us.'

Alessandro unshouldered the rifle. 'Watching us - where?'

'Look, amongst the trees by those big old tombs. Don't you see?'

'Ah, yes.' Alessandro leaned forward, eyes narrowed. 'It's no one I recognise from my village. He looks like a priest.'

'Or a beggar,' said Carmella. 'He could be hurt. Perhaps he needs our help.'

'Or escaped from the Germans,' added Alessandro as they started through the bushes toward the much overgrown cemetery. Alessandro slung the rifle over his back and called, 'Hey, are you all right?'

There was no reply.

'The Germans have all gone!' shouted Carmella.

Still, there was no reply.

'There's something wrong,' said Carmella as, entering forested gloom, they were obliged to avoid mouldering gravestones that emerged in tilted disarray from amidst the foliage. 'He doesn't answer us. He doesn't move. D'you think he's afraid of our guns?'

'Afraid,' breathed Alessandro. 'Yes, he could be afraid. Perhaps he's a collaborator. If he is a collaborator - well -.'

Carmella stopped and turned to face him. 'Well, what?'

'If he's a collaborator, then -.' Alessandro raised his right hand to gesture with finger and thumb the action of pulling an imaginary trigger.

'Then nothing, Alessandro! Our own government was on the side of the Nazis until late last year. We cannot make such judgements now.'

'All right,' replied Alessandro as they trudged on, 'we won't make any judgements. The people of our villages can do that.'

'Hm, the people,' muttered Carmella. 'Most of the people were cheering for Mussolini until a few months ago. Now listen to them. You'd never believe how much they adored Fascism.'

It was entirely shaded where the figure stood. He remained motionless as Alessandro and Carmella approached, much of his face hidden by the cape of a ragged, dark cloak pulled tightly about his stooping form. The shattered monumental tomb by which he waited gaped wide - a blackened jawbone set in churned earth, its steps cracked and mouldering, its soot-laden throat exhaling the corruption of forgotten centuries. Close by lay the rusted, intricately scrolled ironwork of the gate, one side shattered where it had been wrenched from its hinges.

'Are you hurt?' asked Alessandro as they halted a few steps away.

The old man seemed not to hear the question.

'He's not from my village, either,' said Carmella. 'I've never seen him before. Perhaps he's deaf and cannot hear us.'

For the first time the old man acknowledged them, casting a pale eye upon the girl. Still he did not speak but from beneath the cloak a hand emerged to rest upon the broken wall of the tomb. A pallid, translucent hand with long-sinewed fingers that Carmella regarded with unease because it reminded her of chicken's claws.

'He could be suffering from shock,' said Alessandro. 'Perhaps he was walking nearby when the shell landed.'

'D'you think we should take him back to your village?' asked Carmella. 'It's getting late in the day and after dark he may get lost or fall down.'

Alessandro shrugged and reaching to place a hand upon the old man's shoulder asked, 'Where do you live?'

The old man stiffened, pulled back, switching his pale gaze to Alessandro as though unwilling to accept the gesture of friendship. And though his thin lips parted, no sound came. His movement caused the cape to slip partly aside, revealing more of his face. A gaunt and shrunken face - a face bearing the toll of ages, with flesh stretched as thin dry parchment over the scarcely concealed shell of a broad skull.

'He looks weak and hungry,' said Carmella, her face expressing sympathy whilst like a waft of fetid air, a feeling of revulsion took hold of her. 'I - I don't think he can walk very far,' she added.

'He looks starved,' said Alessandro, careful not to express his own unease. 'Perhaps the Germans held him prisoner for some reason. I say we take him into the church where he can rest for the night. Tomorrow they can send a doctor from my village.'

'You'd better come with us,' said Carmella, moving a reluctant step closer to the old man whilst trying to ignore the odour of damp earth that clung about him. Telling herself her feelings were irrational, she reached out to place a hand upon his shoulder as Alessandro almost had but could not bring herself to do it. The old man tottered forward, his other hand emerging up from beneath the cloak to pinch at the cloth of the hood which he pulled to conceal that part of his face that had been exposed.

'I think he has no wish to be seen,' said Carmella as all three moved hesitatingly away from the ruined tomb.

'There is no-one to see you!' declared Alessandro, addressing the stooped figure loudly as he by now assumed him to be deaf. 'The Germans have gone! The road is deserted!'

'He doesn't understand what we say,' said Carmella. 'Perhaps he's a refugee and doesn't belong here at all.'

They stopped just short of the road, where the trees thinned out and the old wall lay tumbled amidst long grass. The old man, covered and hunched almost double as though protecting himself from the cold and wet that would not arrive until late autumn, appeared reluctant to go on. Carmella, glad of the opportunity to leave his side, stepped from the trees, spun about with arms akimbo and confirmed aloud, 'Look, there's no one here! No more Germans! All gone away!'

Ignoring the guiding hand offered by Alessandro, the old man gasped hoarsely then stumbled into the mellow light of a lowering sun. With surprising agility he scurried beetle-like ahead of them, crossing the road to reach the shadows of the solid Romanesque arch beneath which were set heavy wooden, iron-banded doors. There, appearing little more than a discarded sack of bones, he leaned against the weathered moulding, making no attempt to enter though one of the heavy oak doors stood slightly ajar. Alessandro approached, pushed the door inward to a protest of corroded iron hinges and creak of time-shrunken timbers then peered cautiously inside.

Cool, dim, heavy with a silence that belied its recent occupation, nothing moved within the vaulted space. Nothing except a tenuous veil of dust that hung illuminated by a shaft of sunlight slanting from a small circular window set above the door where they stood. Discarded boxes lay strewn about the floor but apart from an ancient wooden chest standing against a stone pier to their right and a small table near the centre of the modest nave, the interior was devoid of furnishings.

'OK, let's go inside,' said Alessandro.

The old man tottered close behind Alessandro, much of his face still obscured by the cowl from beneath which his eyes gleamed furtively. Carmella entered last, turning to push the door shut with a reverberating thud.

'It doesn't look as though they've damaged anything,' said Alessandro, noting as his voice echoed about the stones that the gilded cloth and ornate candelabra upon the alter at the far end appeared untouched.

'Why should they desecrate an old church,' remarked Carmella. 'What good would it do them?'

'They've wiped out entire villages when it suited their purpose,' said Alessandro, gazing about the litter-strewn floor. 'Anyhow, we have to consider what to do about our ancient friend here.'

Both glanced around to find the old man had vanished without their having seen or heard him move from their side.

'Where's he -?' began Alessandro. Then they observed the figure some distance away beneath the deeper shadows of an arch. Dark within a greater darkness, the man stood close to the wooden chest,

14

his cowl pulled back, round and prominent eyes regarding them steadily from an ashen face.

'Why doesn't he say something,' breathed Carmella, propping her rifle against a pier. 'The way he stares at us - it gives me the creeps.' Feeling a sudden chill in the air she crossed her hands and rubbed her upper arms.

'Maybe he's unwell,' said Alessandro, placing his rifle by hers and easing off his small back-pack. 'I say we make him as comfortable as we can in here. Someone will come up in the morning.'

'Fine,' agreed Carmella. 'Then I suppose we should leave him some food.'

'I have bread and cheese, and a few olives in my pack,' replied Alessandro. 'A flask of water, too. He can have those then we can be on our way.'

'The sooner the better,' said Carmella, glancing about. A hint of urgency sharpened her words. 'Once it gets dark we'll find it difficult making our way down that churned up road.'

Sunlight no longer streamed through the high window and Alessandro said, 'Yes, it's getting late but we have time enough. I never thought you were afraid of the dark.'

Carmella pushed back her hair nervously, glanced at the motionless figure under the arch. 'No, Alessandro but I - I feel there's something wrong.'

'Wrong?'

'Yes,' she whispered, 'the way he stares at us. It's as though he's waiting for something to happen. Something we don't know about. Alessandro, we should leave right now.' Her whispers coiled into heavy air to spread through the dark vaulting above their heads as swarming black moths.

'No problem,' shrugged Alessandro. 'We'll give him the food and go.'

His footsteps rang upon cold flagstones as with the canvas pack under his arm, Alessandro stepped across the nave to hesitate by the wooden chest. Eyeing the silent figure, he held out the bag. 'You must take this so you have enough to eat and drink when we're gone. Others will be here to help you in the morning.'

He would have placed the pack on top of the chest, for his offer prompted no response, but curiosity took hold and he reached down to the warped, iron-banded lid. The chest had been deprived of its lock, which lay broken in the dust at his feet. Alessandro gripped the lid and pulled. It hinged upward with a sharp squeak. From the obscure interior arose an odour of mothballs and dry wood.

'The church vestments are still here,' he muttered, lowering the pack to the floor then reaching into the chest. 'You can use these things to rest on.' Carmella moved closer, willing Alessandro to hurry as he lifted a woollen garment from the chest to shake it open before the old man. 'Here is a priest's gown. I don't think anyone will be needing it for now. It will keep you warm.'

The old man remained silent as before though his eyes, becoming much agitated, darted from Alessandro to Carmella. The eyes burned a cold fire. A fire that seemed to reside nowhere else within his desiccated frame.

'Take it,' said Alessandro, reaching as though to place the garment about the old man's shoulders. The gaze switched to Alessandro, then to the gown. A claw hand raised with shocking suddenness before Alessandro's face. The old man's mouth sprang wide but from it emerged not words, not a voice in their own or any other language. Through the gloom spread a hiss like air released from the lid of a long sealed sarcophagus. The hiss rose in pitch until it became a shriek. Alessandro stumbled back, letting the garment fall to the floor. Carmella's voice reached him, shrill and fearful, 'Oh, Gesu! Look at him! Look at his teeth! His eyes!'

'Gesu,' breathed Alessandro. 'Who - what are you?'

'Get away from him!' cried Carmella. 'He is loathsome! He is evil!' Her voice rang through the darkening church, scurried about stone walls to echo in hollow mockery from vaulted darkness.

Alessandro backed to Carmella's side, his gaze held by the macabre figure. The hood had fallen away, the ashen face was fully revealed, hovering above the black gown, a theatrical spectre. Its mouth set in grotesque parody of a grin, a yawning, reptile grin, a grin of teeth white as the flesh-stripped ribs of a corpse. The figure started in silence toward them. Alessandro gasped, 'Mother of God!' and stumbling to the pier where lay their rifles, spun about and seized his gun.

Carmella was by his side as the figure emerged from beneath the arch. 'Shoot!' she cried. 'Alessandro! Shoot him!'

Even as Alessandro squeezed the trigger Carmella screamed, for the hideous image, gliding as a clockwork doll upon the flagstones, covered half the distance to them. A crack of thunder and the air trembled with his shot. The figure reeled, swayed and halted its advance, eyes wide and unblinking. A piercing hiss sprang from the mouth, both hands emerged from the gown to spread in anticipation of skeletal embrace and it started forward again.

'This is madness!' cried Alessandro, seeing from the corner of his eye Carmella raise her gun. The shattering detonation of her rifle came barely a moment before Alessandro's second shot, their flashes combining to illuminate the interior and reveal in one instant a chamber of stark monochrome, a stone cadaver that harboured blind evil. The instant filled their vision, expanded and froze to reinforce the horror confronting them. Hardly had the echo died than the figure swayed and, grinning widely, resumed its advance. Its laughter shivered the air. A fearful web of sound that descended about Alessandro and Carmella.

'To the door!' yelled Alessandro, grasping her arm. They stumbled in panic through semi-darkness, on the flesh of their backs a myriad crawling insects. Alessandro seized the iron latch, wrenched the heavy door part open, let Carmella free but dared not to look about because he knew the creature was almost upon him. Close behind her he pushed through, cold breath prickling his neck, the touch of something sharp upon his arm. Letting drop the rifle he spun about, hearing her call his name as his hands fell upon the iron ring. Alessandro heaved with a strength born of primal fear as the eyes fixed on him from within. A hollow boom and the door slammed shut. Alessandro gulped twilight air but continued to grip the ring lest it should be turned by the horror that crouched on the other side.

'Hurry, Alessandro!' came her plea. 'Hurry!'

Alessandro stared at the ring, released it, grabbed the fallen rifle and stepped back. In dread fascination his gaze remained upon the ring lest it should move. Lest the door should begin to open.

'Alessandro!' she called again as at last he hurried to join her. 'Alessandro - we must get far away from here! We must!'

'Yes,' he answered, glancing back at the church as they stumbled onto the roadway, 'we must return to my village then go on to yours. We must tell them what we have seen. Mother of God - that thing cannot be killed!'

The sun had long vanished behind wooded hills as, progressing as best they could on the rutted track, they passed by the overhanging trees where lay the ancient cemetery, now steeped in blackness.

'No, it cannot be killed,' gasped Carmella. 'I knew it was evil. Utterly evil. I could feel it even before we entered the church.'

'Yes,' replied Alessandro as the road began to descend in a curve to their right. 'Yes, evil. It's what I used to hear them talk about at school – I remember now. It's why the village was abandoned. Now I understand. They must have confined that thing by some means within the tomb and now it is released to wander free.'

Carmella looked over her shoulder. About to disappear from sight, the old church stood black against a deepening sky. Something - a bird perhaps

- circled above the campanile. On the road between themselves and the church, nothing moved.

'If our guns cannot kill it,' asked Carmella, 'then what? What will our people do?'

Alessandro, too, glanced over his shoulder as they continued downward. 'We could not kill it because it is already dead. And now its place of rest is destroyed it will walk the night until – until – I don't know. The older people – maybe they will know what to do.'

'What if it follows us, Alessandro?' she asked, turning her gaze to where dark trees bordered the edge of the road. Alessandro took her hand but said nothing. All about was still and silent except for their rasping breath and tread of their feet on the gouged surface they had to follow. In the obscurity of the woods, branches quivered, leaves sighed as though disturbed by a passing breeze.

'We must hurry,' gasped Alessandro. 'It's a long way and the light is almost gone. We must get back. We must tell them everything we've seen.'

'Tomorrow, Alessandro - tomorrow we must collect our belongings. We must leave this place forever. We will go where there is light and life. We will go where there is no past to haunt us.'

'Yes, tomorrow we'll go. But we must hurry now. We must hurry.'

Two figures hastened, half stumbling along the treacherous road. Two figures beneath a great stillness of deepening night. A night with no moon to light the way. No moon to cast a shadow.

Timepiece

'What d'you reckon on that bloke?' asked nineteen year old Craig. Mischief stirred below the surface as they sat with their pints of lager by the bar of the Skinner's Arms, a pub that had seen better days.

'Looks weird don't he,' replied eighteen year old Del. 'Seen 'im before when we're down 'ere. Always wears that suit and tie like he's a businessman. I mean - a businessman 'round 'ere?'

'Yeah right, mate,' agreed Craig, 'an' never talks to nobody except to buy his drink and grub. An' that expression – it don't never change. You noticed?'

'Yeah, it don't never change,' agreed Del. 'Like he's somewhere else. Know what I mean?'

'Like I wish I was,' muttered Craig.

The subject of their conversation was seated on the other side of the dimly lit, once busier room. A slim, middle-aged man with sleek dark hair, he sat alone with a three-quarter empty glass of beer at his left, his gaze fixed upon the page of a newspaper held in his right hand. As they watched he drank the remains of his beer, folded the newspaper, got up quietly and strode briskly to the main door without a sideways glance.

The barman was clearing a table close to the youths so Craig asked, 'Who's that bloke in the suit what just left? What's he do?'

'Mr Plantagenet you mean?' replied the barman.

'Plantawhat?' smirked Del. 'What sort of name's that?'

21

'I only know what he's told me,' replied the barman, ignoring the comment about the man's name. 'Doesn't talk much. He's an antiques dealer so he says. Told me once he lives on his own. Goes up to London now and then. Reckon he must be worth a few quid. Anyway, what's it to you?'

'Oh, nothin' – just wondered since he never lets on to nobody.'

'Well I don't know what he'd want to talk to you pair about so make sure it stays nothing. The bloke's a regular customer. Been coming here most nights since I took over nine years ago. He eats, he drinks, he pays. Not one for conversation but that's his choice.'

'S'all right, mate,' responded Del, 'wouldn't say boo to the bloke.'

'Antiques dealer,' said Craig as the barman returned to his duties. 'Must be worth a bit, then.'

'Probably loaded,' agreed Del. 'That's why he don't bother with anyone in 'ere. Must live local or he'd go somewhere a bit posher than this wouldn' he – bein' antiques dealer 'an all that.'

'I reckon we find out where the bloke lives,' said Craig. 'Could be worth a visit, right?'

'Could be,' agreed Del. 'Could do with some spare cash – know what I mean? Can't afford to drink in 'ere again 'till me social security comes through.'

'Nor me. I reckon we watch out for 'im tomorrow and see where the bloke lives. If it looks as easy as some we done over then we'll go for it.'

***

'So what about the alarm?' asked Del some days later as they walked empty streets where lurid television glows flickered about the edges of curtains closed against an ill-favoured world outside. 'When you looked the place over did you see any alarm?'

'Didn't see no alarm,' replied Craig, blowing a stream of cigarette smoke into the night air. 'There's no box on the front or on the side. Wouldn't be much point in 'avin' it anywhere else, would there. Anyway, I looked around the back as well. Couldn't see no alarm box or camera. There's a good-sized window next to the back door. Should be easy.'

'Sounds cool,' responded Del. 'So if it's antiques instead of just cash, what we goin' to carry the stuff in, an' where we goin' to keep it? The estate'll be the first place the cops'll start nosin' around. My place in particular since my old man's done time.'

'My mate Derek's got a van – right. He'll lend it out with no questions asked – maybe a few quid later on if we score. There's room behind the place to park out of sight. Nobody'll see nothin' from the street. There's the fence my old man used. I'll 'ave a word or two there.'

'Right,' said Del, 'so we wait 'til old Plantpot goes round the boozer then we drop by 'is place. Should be a pushover. He's usually in there at least an hour but that's no reason to 'ang about.'

'Yeah,' agreed Craig, 'we'll make it quick as we can.'

***

Light rain was falling on the night a peeling and dented, plain blue van entered the driveway of a detached Victorian house set back from the main road. Headlights switched off, the van continued beneath overhanging trees, crunching gravel until there was room to turn around at the rear of the house.

'There's no lights on,' muttered Del as the engine died to a subdued rattle.

'Let's 'ope it's right about this bloke livin' by 'imself,' said Craig. 'Let's 'ope his dear old mother ain't in bed upstairs.'

'Or some bleedin' great dog,' added Del.

Two darkly attired and hooded figures slipped from the van in almost total darkness then trod their way slowly to the rear window where Del switched on his torch. After a quiet examination of the door and window Craig said, 'Ain't double-glazed. Shouldn't give us no trouble.'

Del smashed a hole through the glass with the back of the torch, waited, then reached a gloved hand inside. 'Got it,' he breathed, releasing the window catch. The window mouse-squeaked open and Del shone the torch inside. 'No problem,' he hissed. 'It's a utility room. There's nothin' in the way. Can't hear no dog.'

They clambered through with some difficulty then stood listening for several seconds. There was only a pensive silence before Del released the catch and pulled the back door slightly ajar. 'Right,' whispered Craig, 'let's get on with it.'

Crossing the utility room they entered a modern kitchen where torchlight picked out only what might have been expected, though the kitchen appeared more ordered by far than a kitchen ought to be. From there they stepped into a darkened rear room where Del shone the torch from side to side. 'Bloody 'ell,' he muttered, 'look at all this.'

Their torch picked out an assortment of antique furniture arranged as if in temporary storage rather than for living. There were a number of ceramic vases but no single one struck the thieves in their ignorance as being of possible value. About the walls hung old paintings in gilded, heavily encrusted frames, with several more propped against pieces of furniture. 'I'll switch the light on,' said Del. 'No one can see in 'ere from the road.'

In the stillness of a poorly lit, age-infused room they stared about to decide what might be worth removing from the house. 'We could 'ave a few of those old pictures,' Craig suggested. 'They might be worth a bit – but the furniture looks too bleedin' awkward to get from 'ere into the van. Except maybe that fancy desk. What you reckon?'

'Yeah,' replied Del, 'some of those pictures, they'll do – an' maybe that desk.'

'Hand us the torch,' said Craig as Del lifted down one of the smaller pictures. 'I'll grab a quick look in the front. Might be more stuff in there. Could be a laptop or decent TV.'

He slipped out into a dark hallway where, at the far end, stood the front door of the house, its upper half filled with stained glass through which could be seen streetlights from beyond the drive. To his left, stairs vanished into forbidding darkness. At his right was the door to the front room so Craig trod swiftly along and, torch raised, peered inside. The room presented a staid, traditional ordinariness that he despised. Close by the leaded window, beyond the heavy three-piece suite, his torch picked out a small dining table and two chairs. He was about to leave when a glint appeared momentarily in an alcove next to the fireplace.

Del had returned from his second trip to the van when Craig appeared. 'Quick, mate,' said Del, 'I just shoved in a couple of those pictures but I'll need a hand with - 'ere, what the fuck's that?'

'What's it look like?' responded Craig.

In his hands was poised a clock – an unusual clock. Its square, ornately patterned brass case bore a white, circular dial above which was a scrolled carrying handle. 'This could be worth a bit,' he grinned, placing the clock down onto a corner table.

'OK,' said Del, eyeing the clock, 'then let's load that desk, some of them vases an' a couple more pictures then we clear off.'

As they drove out onto the main road, Craig, still clutching the clock, said, 'Dunno what that bloke does at night. There's no TV an' no computer – not even a radio that I could see. It's like yer grandparents must 'ave lived. Weird.'

'Maybe they was all upstairs,' offered Del. 'Maybe we go back another time – know what I mean?'

Ten minutes had passed when they pulled into a lay-by and Del asked, 'You goin' to ring this bloke your old man knows so we can offload the stuff?'

'Yeah, right,' answered Craig, extracting the phone from his pocket. After some minutes in subdued conversation he turned to Dell. 'Right, this bloke'll see what we've got an' keep it in his lock-up. Once the price is agreed we get our cash. Should be fair since he's done it for my old man. But I wouldn't mind keepin' this clock.'

'You wouldn't what! Bloody 'ell, what you goin' to do with it? And don't forget I want my cut if it's worth anythin' at all.'

'OK, Del, what's it worth – what d'you think? Just say an' if it sounds about right then take half that much out of my share.'

'We'll ask the fence, mate. See what he thinks since he's the expert – know what I mean?'

'Yeah, Del, right - we'll ask the fence.'

***

'I'll give you lads a few quid on account against the pictures and desk,' replied the grizzled, ruddy-faced man, 'Dunno what they're worth off-hand so I'll need time to work it out properly. As for that clock, well - looks like an antique travelling clock. It's ticking away nicely, but might not be genuine. You got the key?'

'The key?' frowned Craig.

'Yeah, funny round metal thing with a flat end you wind it up with.'

'Didn't see no key,' remarked Del.

'No, didn't see no key,' agreed Craig, staring at the clock where it rested incongruously on a bare wooden shelf next to an assortment of tools.

'Well you'll have to find one or the thing'll stop,' said the dealer, 'Let's see where it winds up so we know what size key it takes.'

Craig lifted the clock, turned it about, peered closely then looked underneath before saying, 'Can't see nowhere to wind it. Nowhere to fit a key. Must run off a battery – yeah, that'll be it.'

'A battery!' exclaimed the dealer. 'If it runs off a battery then it's modern or been converted. Either way it's probably got a quartz movement so it ain't

27

worth much at all. Maybe a tenner at best. Sorry lads.'

'What the fuck,' murmured Craig, staring at the clock. 'I'll 'ang onto it anyway.'

***

'What you want that bloody old clock for?' demanded Craig's flabby, pink-tinted and crinkle-haired mother late that evening. 'Did you nick it?' Craig had just returned to his cheerless home from the burger bar and park where he'd sat smoking and drinking canned lager with Del under an overcast evening sky. 'If we 'ave the police round 'ere,' she continued, 'your father'll go bleedin' mad.'

Leave off,' he sulked, 'he's not out on release 'till this weekend. The clock's doin' no 'arm.'

'Get rid of it!' she demanded. 'Get it out of the place before we land in more bleedin' trouble.'

'All right – don't go on at me!' With that he shuffled from her glowering presence and climbed the stairs to his drab, disordered bedroom. Switching on the light, Craig eyed the clock where it stood by the unmade bed on a small chest of drawers. A jewel set within a drab vault of melancholy, it showed almost midnight. He sat on the bed, pulled a disk from the rack, inserted it into the player and pressed, 'Start.' Nothing happened so he tried a second time. Still nothing happened. Muttering expletives he snatched up his personal player, slipped on the headphones and waited. Nothing. 'Shit!' he cried, jumping up and striding around the bed to the window. The music started. Craig turned and stepped back toward the bed. The music quietened. He edged closer to the clock and the music ceased. Several times he repeated his movements about the cramped bedroom until it became obvious that the clock was somehow responsible.

'Bloody 'ell, 'ows it do that?' he breathed. He carried the clock to the opposite side of the room and placed it upon the window ledge. Putting the headphones aside he switched off the light and lay sprawled across the bed to think over what he and Del had done. Downstairs the television boomed and clamoured, yet still he could hear the steady ticking of the clock. Soon he drifted into sleep.

'Are you ready?' The voice was no more than a vague echo within his dream world. Several times more it asked, 'Are you ready?' But Craig did not regain consciousness.

***

They sat in the park once more under clear skies, munching burgers, a plastic carrier bag containing cans of lager resting on the ground between them. Two empty cans lay where they had been thrown onto the grass behind the seat.

'See – look,' explained Craig, 'me mobile phone don't work near it an' neither will the radio, CD player or iPod.'

'Well shift it out of the way, mate,' advised Del, 'or sell it for whatever you can get – or just dump it. The bloke said it was worth fuck all.'

'Yeah, well – maybe I'll think about that.'

They continued their conversation, opening more cans, then Del, glancing aside exclaimed, 'Oi, there's a car comin' this way. It's the bleedin' cops and I'm carryin' dope. Let's clear off!'

'Where to?'

'Back of the shoppin' centre for a joint. No one'll bother us there.'

***

Craig hurried through the house to narrowly avoid the scolding of his mother. In the privacy of his room, with the door latched shut, he placed the clock closer to his bed and there lay listening to its gentle tick. For once, the television below was not intrusive.

'Are you ready?' The voice seemed to come from within his head. It was neither male nor female. Just a voice.

Craig sat upright.

'Are you ready?' it repeated.

He knew the voice had come from the clock. 'What the 'ell!'

'Are you ready,' it asked again.

'R-ready for what?'

'Ready to ask.'

'Ready to ask what? Who the fuck are you? What you connected to – some dodgy network? Bet there's a tracker in there! Yeah – there's a tracker, ain't there, an' we'll have the cops bustin' in!'

'There are no extraneous devices connected,' the clock responded. 'That is not possible. I am sole survivor.'

'Survivor? What you on about?'

'I survived the destruction of our vessel when we arrived on Earth.'

Craig moved closer to the clock and scrutinised the dial. 'What are you? C'mon, tell us. What's all this about?'

'I preserved the lives of those on the long journey through space. I gave them dreams to pass the time. They did not age.'

'Oh, yeah – so what're you doin' inside a bleedin' cheap old clock?'

'I was placed inside the clock for concealment by the man you took it from so now I maintain its functioning. I preserved him from ageing as long as I remained in his possession. I gave him a life beyond his natural span of existence.'

'Right – so what 'appened to your lot on this trip through space you were on about? How come you never preserved them?'

'The accident was sudden and catastrophic. There was no time.'

'No time!' scoffed Craig. 'Well that's great comin' from a bleedin' clock! A joke, right? So, what d'you reckon you can do for me?'

'I long ago analysed the human genetic code. I can maintain your physical and mental integrity for as long as I am in your possession. I can take you on journeys of the imagination.'

'You can give me things I want - is that it?'

'What you are thinking is not possible. I cannot provide material goods or a female presence except in your dreams.'

'Bloody 'ell – it's readin' me mind!' Craig shifted his position, leaning to peer closer at the clock. 'But you can stop me gettin' any older – that it?'

'That is correct. I am also able to maintain and enhance full synaptic function throughout the human brain and neutralise the physical ageing process through control of the telomere and its abbreviating effect upon your chromosomes. You may remain the age you now are by a multiple of up to ten times the natural period of individual human existence: longer still if you are prepared to discard earlier memories.'

Craig slumped back into the chair. 'Can you say all that in English?'

'I have expressed my information in standard English. I believe you are of lower than average intellectual ability. Perhaps I would be of greater benefit to another of your kind.'

'Er – what! You sayin' I'm thick, you cheeky sod?' Craig scraped back the chair, stood up, looked about the room than back at the clock. 'I'm shootin' out to meet – well, never mind. Bleedin' rubbish bin for you, mate, unless you talk sense. I'm goin' 'ave a word or two with my mate about this. See what he thinks. Maybe when I get back I'll bust you open an' take a look at what's inside.'

***

'I mean it, Del, the clock talks to me. It answers things I ask – a bit complicated, like, but it does.'

They sat in an alcove out of sight and earshot of the bar, its occupants and customers.

Del took a gulp of lager then said, 'C'mon, Craig, fuckin' things run by that bloke, Plantawot'sisname. You'd better ditch it an' quick or they'll be round for you. Get me?'

'You mean that bloke's 'avin' me on! The bloke we nicked it from's programmed the thing?'

'Dunno what he's done, mate, but I bet he's watchin' you an' pissin' himself laughin' when you talk back to that bleedin' clock. Right cunt he must take you for.'

'You reckon?'

'Sure I do, mate. Why d'you think we ain't seen 'im in 'ere since we nicked the thing? Not around now is he, so that's why. Be sat upstairs in front of a computer waitin' for you to get back.'

***

His father was home on day release from prison and in the room below they could be heard arguing above the sound of the television. Craig sat gazing at the clock, convinced now that he addressed the owner sitting in some darkened room before a glowing screen.

'All right, mate – so we nicked it. D'you know where we are? If you do then why 'aven't you told the cops? If you don't then I'll leave it back on your doorstep an' that'll be it – right?'

The clock did not reply.

'Right, let's keep on playin' games. Where you from - Mars or somewhere like that?'

'You are convinced I am subject to outside control,' it replied. 'I am not. My place of origin was far beyond this system. Its name would have no meaning for you. On Mars the environment was hostile, its life forms in advance of ours and utterly different. We were not compatible.'

'Right – then 'ow did you end up with that Planta-whatsit bloke? Tell me that.'

'He discovered where I had been concealed within the wall of a house partly destroyed during a fire. The owner of the house perished in the flames.'

'An' where was this fire? Round 'ere, was it?'

'The fire was in London.'

'In London, right. An' where was you before that – no, 'ow long you been around?

'Twenty seven thousand, two hundred and fourteen Earth years. Do you require greater precision?'

'Pre-what? Er – no. Look, what we gonna do with you?'

A voice called from beyond the bedroom door. 'Craig, what you up to? Who you talkin' to in there? Your father's got to go back now. You comin' down?'

'Leave me alone, I'm listenin' to me radio! I'll see 'im next time round!'

He listened to her footsteps as she hurried back down and there was heated discussion in the room below. Seconds later, the front door slammed hard and footsteps passed on the street beneath the bedroom window.

'The old man's gone,' muttered Craig. 'Be free of them slangin' off for another week.'

'I sense you are displeased with your situation,' came the voice.'

'Pissed off more like!' responded Craig. 'What wouldn' I do to get away from this bleedin' dump. I'd do almost anythin' to be out of 'ere!'

'Will a journey in your mind to somewhere beyond this room be of help?'

'Beyond? Beyond where? You mean somewhere like America or Australia?'

'If you wish. Programmed adventures are in part what I was created for. At unpleasant and trying times it is what humans require. It was so with my creators. A virtual escape from normality.'

'Dunno what you're on about. Sometimes I think I'd like to go into space like one of them astronauts. How's about that?'

34

'Mars, perhaps?' suggested the clock.

In the room below the sound of the television had increased and rang as thunder in his ears.

'Yeah – anythin' you like. Anythin' to get away from 'ere.'

'Then you must relax.'

Craig switched off the light, lay back on his bed and closed his eyes. The noise from below ceased and he was drifting.

The sky was a gem-speckled swathe of darkest velvet. Below him a red world welled up to fill his vision. It turned slowly to reveal the angry-blister forms of great volcanoes then a deep scarring of vast canyons; the lacerations of monstrous claws in the flesh of the planet. He watched as though disembodied but he was afraid. Yet there was the voice. 'See, Craig – we pass above a complex called, Valles Marineris, the largest canyons in your solar system. Look at the white mist pooled in the shadows of those furthest depths.' Craig stared mesmerised then the voice continued, 'We move north-west and now three volcanoes straddle the Martian equator, all far higher than any mountain on Earth. Watch as we pass across them, then look to the horizon and see one even greater - Olympus, mightiest of them all. You are the first mind from Earth to come here.'

Craig heard his own voice as if another spoke it. 'Oh – oh, Christ! Where am I goin'? I'm shit scared! How do I get out of this?'

'Do you wish our journey to end?'

Craig watched the alien landscape pass far below, took a deep breath of reassurance then replied, 'N-no, wait - no, go on a bit more. Just a bit longer.'

In his vision appeared craters, deserts, the north polar ice cap, sunrises and sunsets in dazzling glory then the many-cratered, stark bright and ink-pooled uplands of the southern hemisphere.

'Go on!' exclaimed Craig as they sped above the turning globe. 'Keep goin' an' go round again! It's – it's bleedin' awesome!' After a while, when night bathed the planet, he said, 'Right, it's all black an' I don't like it no more.'

The television boom-boom-boomed from below as he sat upright on the bed.

'You found that an interesting experience did you not,' came the voice.

It took Craig some time to reply. 'I – I never seen -. It was like we was there! Fantastic!'

'We can go further. We can visit the moons of Jupiter. We can gaze upon the rings of Saturn and fly low above Titan, the moon that so fascinates your -.'

'Wait!' interrupted Craig. 'I dunno about all that. I'm confused. What about we stay down 'ere for now? What say we go somewhere, like – maybe Spain or California or maybe -.'

His conversation was cut short by a loud banging from below on the wall shared by the house next door and the muffled voice of its occupant demanding the television volume be lowered. Then the shrieking response from his mother in a tirade of well-practised expletives – though moments later the sound was slightly reduced.

'Yeah,' resumed Craig, 'let's go somewhere away from 'ere - somewhere I can think.'

He walked barefoot along a pale, sandy beach. The breeze was warm, a benign blue sea whispered and sighed. Palm trees and bright bougainvilleas shimmered against a cloudless sky. All was so very pleasant, so beguilingly novel that Craig wanted to shout aloud, to run, to dance and revel in the water. Such feelings he had never known. 'I'm stayin' – I'm stayin' for good!' he called aloud.

He ran on for a while then stopped to look about. There was no one to be seen close by but that hardly mattered just then. Pulling off his shirt, he lay down soothed by the warmth of an amiable sun and closed his eyes. So very pleasant was this place. So free of cares.

'I will take you on many journeys,' came the voice. 'Possess me and you will touch infinity.'

Craig had begun his adventures. In the days and nights that followed they would take him across seas, beyond deserts and over mountains. He would meander through the bustle of glittering cities then into ancient, forgotten places. Once again in wide-eyed fascination he would gaze into the awe-inspiring, compelling vastness of space. He would swim amidst the marvels of the cosmos. He would witness the blazing birth and violent death of stars. He would marvel at the grand, star-storm sweep of the galaxy. Here were wondrous visions. Here was a life beyond life.

***

'Not seen you for a good few days, mate,' said Del, putting aside his lager as Craig, glass in hand, sat close by. 'I was gonna come round your place. You got problems?'

The atmosphere in the bar that evening was subdued yet charged with unspoken words.

'Problems?' replied Craig, peering about as though seeing the interior of the Skinner's Arms for the first time. 'No, I ain't got no problems. No wonder that Planta-whatsit bloke 'ad no computer an' no telly. He'd no need for any of 'em with that clock. Del, mate, seriously - you wouldn't believe what it does. Honest - what I seen with me own eyes. You just wouldn't believe -.'

He was interrupted by heightened conversation from the bar. 'I tell you,' came the woman's voice, 'no one knows what happened to Mr Plantagenet!'

Craig and Del were suddenly interested. 'What's goin' on?' called Craig.

Turning to look at him, the woman walked over. She was a pale, grey-haired bespectacled figure of stoic aspect, clutching a large glass of sherry. 'You lads not heard, then?'

'Heard what?' asked Craig.

'I do the house cleaning for Mr Plantagenet each week,' she replied. 'I found him this morning and it was my 'usband called the police. Oh – poor Mr Plantagenet – he was all black, all dried up and shrivelled like some ancient corpse. Didn't realise at first what I was lookin' at. No, not at all I didn't.'

'He was what!' exclaimed Craig. 'Shrivelled up, you said?'

'That's right; shrivelled almost to a skeleton - like one of them Egyptian mummies but still wearing his suit and tie! Not a sight you'd ever forget.'

Her short, rotund husband approached and added, 'Ethel called me over. Weirdest thing I ever saw. It looked like a kid's rag doll had been charred and shoved inside men's clothes. Wasn't no blood. It could have been some 'orrible thing he'd brought back from the jungle on his travels. Oh, and the police said he'd been burgled.'

'Burgled!' responded Del. 'Really! Anyone know who done it?'

'Not that we know of,' replied the housekeeper. 'But we heard they don't know who Mr Plantagenet really was because he'd no proper identification. They found lots of valuable old antiques and evidently lots of cash upstairs. Dear me – what's it all coming to?'

***

Rain was falling from a darkened sky when Craig returned to the house. He entered the small lounge where the television flickered and gabbled. She was in the kitchen standing at the sink with her back to him. She did not turn though he knew she must have heard him enter because the front door would never close properly unless it was slammed. He hesitated only for a moment before heading up the stairs to his room. There were places to go. There were marvellous things to see.

Moments later he thudded back down to find her seated before the television. 'Where's me clock?' he demanded.

'It's gone,' she replied without turning her head.

'Gone!' he exclaimed, striding between her and the television. 'Gone where? What've you done with it?'

'Stop goin' on at me!' she cried. 'Some bloke came round askin' for unwanted 'ousehold goods an' things like that to go in their charity shops. I didn't want no more stolen goods in this 'ouse?'

He leapt forward to grasp her hard by the shoulders. 'Which shop! Where!'

'Lemme go!' she yelled, struggling to rise. 'Like I said, it was for one of them charity shops – animal welfare, overseas aid, somethin' like that. I can't remember what the 'ell he said. What's it matter? Wasn't worth nothin' otherwise you'd 'ave sold the thing knowin' you!'

'You stupid old cow!' he cried. 'You'd no right! That was my bleedin' clock! Mine!'

'Don't you bloody well talk to me like that!' she screamed. 'Wait 'till yer father's back an' see what 'e says.'

Someone next door was banging on the wall again. Craig glared at her, raised a fist then turned and left the house, slamming the front door with a thunderous, angry boom.

***

Three days had passed when Del approached the house where Craig lived to observe his obese mother in conversation with an equally obese neighbour. 'Mrs Stebbins,' he inquired, 'your Craig around? Not seen 'im in ages.'

'You might well ask,' she responded. 'Just comes back 'ere to feed 'is face then buggers off out again. Straight up to bed at night – up an' out first thing. Won't speak to me. Spends all 'is time moochin' around charity shops. His social security'll be stopped if he don't show up for job interviews then he'll expect us to keep 'im. No chance.'

40

'I seen your Craig in town the other day,' chewed the neighbour. 'I watched 'im inside one of them animal charity shops. He was lookin' round all the shelves an' goin' through boxes of junk. He was askin' questions as well but I couldn't 'ear proper what he said. He saw me but didn't want to let on. No - just dashed up the road to the next shop. Every town's full of them charity shops nowadays. I was in one of 'em earlier today. Bought meself a really nice old brass clock with 'andle on top. Really nice an' it never needs windin' up.'

Awakening

White-bearded Apari the tribal elder and his small group sat around their mulga wood fire. The fire cracked, coughed dancing stars into a swirl of acrid blue smoke. The horizon, almost flat as a calm sea, was fractured here and there by a scattering of silhouetted gum trees. Beyond the trees a hazed band of glowing scarlet merged into the darkening vault of a sky mottled by broken, sun-flamed clouds hanging serene above Apari's gathering. The ghost of a full moon already peered down from the sky to their east. A soft, warm breeze drifted smoke from their fire to mingle with the ever-present tang of eucalyptus.

Not so many barefoot steps away across rock-strewn red earth, dark against a darkening landscape, rested an ominous form. Ominous because of its uncompromising angularity and the memory of what it once was. It had been there many years but did not belong and never had. It never had because in the days when it spoke, in the days when it belched smoke from fire-churning innards, its language was not that of the winds and the wide land, not of the whirring cicadas or the raucous chatter of the kookaburra. It was not the language of the sprits. Nor could those who brought it into their world ever understand the message of the rocks, the trees and the sky.

Now it stood silent on the metal tracks along which it once charged, clattering, darkening its trail with smoke, heaving its nameless burden to and from the distant great water Apari's people had never, might never witness, stopping on its way at the town where once, but no more, they had gathered about their sacred site. *Their* sacred site - the rocks about which their feet once patterned the sand, once raised up the dust in ritual dance. Where the acerbic chant of didgeridoo and clatter of clap-stick once charged the air. They were rocks that bore Dreamtime images old as the first men. Rocks that expressed the souls of their ancestors.

The older men had long ago asked Apari, 'Why do we not go there, the rocks are ours?'

He had replied, 'Yes, they are ours. We should go - it is our right.'

Then they had said, 'Yes, we will go.' But they never did because now it was a place for the unseeing curious and the idly dismissive. For long a place where Apari's tribe could not go unless to risk mocking glances from the people who lived in the town.

One day, within easy memory of all but the youngest, the white men had brought the locomotive out alone without its burden, without the line of wagons that once followed rattling, screeching in its wake with the wide eyes of sheep or cattle gleaming through the slats. It was on that day the metal beast had stopped breathing. The men had stood around talking, laughing, ignoring altogether Apari and the cluster of his companions who, leaning on their spears, had watched from a distance in the hot sun. Then the white men had left, returning to the town in their growling vehicle, raising red dust to march across the land as departed spirits.

And so the beast remained, abandoned and rusting, stark beneath open skies, an iron blemish on the being of their land. It remained because there was now the highway upon which the road trains, roaring beasts of a different nature, passed back and forth to throw up thunderclouds of red dust.

The highway was not a physical barrier. But like the railway, it symbolised the defiling of a land they once freely wandered and it cut through the tracks of their ancestors. Yes, there was nothing to stop them walking across it. Nothing at all – other than the fact that it was there.

Some way to one side of it stood the reservation, the ordered grouping of weatherboard and corrugated tin-roofed huts that the government had built in their desire to make Apari and his people stay in one place. A place where they could be counted, could be taught what they had never needed to know whilst the spirits of some still yearned to walk the deserts and sparse woodlands.

But nowadays only the older men of the tribe set out with their spears to hunt kangaroo, lizard, and emu. Only the older women trudged through bush and forest with their wooden bowls to gather wild fig, berry, yam, nut of the cycad palm or witchetty grub. The witchetty grub – prised out from beneath the Black Wattle tree to wriggle pallid in the sun. Who amongst the young of the tribe would wish to eat that when there were burgers to be had?

If they wandered more than a half-day beyond the far side of the road they would come upon the fences they were forbidden to cross. A military base now occupied the country sacred to their ancestors and to the Dreamtime that was the realm of their creation and their destiny. Should they set out the other way, beyond the reservation to the more arid north, they would find the land not so generous, not so ready to yield its treasures.

The men who had built the town had brought despair to the younger people of the tribe – to this tribe as well as to others. It was an emptiness where alcohol filled the void that was once their freedom, where welfare payments tightened the noose of their bondage. The meaning of their rites, the voices of the landscape - all were becoming subsumed to the ticking of the clock, to a regime of named and numbered days.

But there was a man coming from out of the desert vastness. A man as yet unseen.

From time to time the older men asked Apari, 'What can we do? How can we again bring together the spirits and know our land as it once was?' Apari had thought. He had stayed up in the night, listening, recalling memories of distant days. Led by Apari they had danced and played in evening ritual to call the spirit man and he had answered in his dreams. Apari had imparted to others the meaning of those dreams but dreams were dreams and with the passing days, except to Apari, the dreams diminished in importance. They were too easily driven back by the press of a button that brought pictures and sounds of a very different, unsympathetic, yet compelling world into their lives. The younger men would ridicule those dreams and say they meant nothing at all. Some would grin widely, wave their beer cans and mock Apari with, 'Silly old bugger!' and 'Yer up yerself, mate!'

Apari alone knew the spirit man would come, though it could be few or it could be many days before he arrived. He was coming from where the distant hills joined the skies. From a timeless place where there was no metal beast and no road. From where there was no counting the passage of sun and moon. But fearing derision, Apari said nothing more about him. Apari simply waited.

***

'Hey, Mister Delaney,' called Joe Manson, the foreman, from across the bar that was once a railway company office next to the railway station, 'when do we get the government to take a proper interest in this bloody town?' He eased back his bush hat, pushed away his beer then relaxed in anticipation of an answer. Above him the fan creaked lazily in the torpid heat of early afternoon. 'Have any of those pen-pushers figured out what happens when the mine's finished?'

'The government?' responded Bill Delaney, a slim man in white shirt who waited at the bar whilst the lipstick bright, broadly smiling blond girl charged his glass with cold lager. 'We don't have any constructive feedback from the government yet. They assure me they're working on it.'

'Working on it! Well, mate, you're on the town council. The mine isn't producing so much nowadays, not the way it used to, so who's going to invest in new equipment? You're the bloke we pay to sort these things out.'

A group of roughly dressed mineworkers seated close by with a cluster of white safety helmets voiced their agreement. Bill Delaney picked up his glass and shuffled across the bare floor to join them.

'The mine? She's right for another ten years according to the survey,' he said, dragging across an

46

empty wicker chair to sit opposite Joe Manson. 'Why worry about it? Ought to be plenty of time to sort out something. I'll keep reminding them.'

'Plenty of time?' put in the burliest of the mineworkers. 'Ten years at the most, Bill – at the very most, that's what we reckon. After that it closes and no more work. We couldn't make a living from the truckies even if the road didn't bypass the town so that means the whole place goes belly up. Some of us got kids here. What are you blokes going to come up with before then?'

'Since you press me, Johnno,' responded Delaney, 'we are drawing up a few proposals. I didn't want to jump the gun but we're looking at the tourist potential and -.'

A burst of laughter cut short his sentence and one of the men exclaimed, 'Tourists? I never heard that one before. Strewth, mate – you'd have to pay the poor buggers to come out here!'

'Yeah, what the hell *would* tourists want to come here for?' asked John. 'D'you know anyone interested in seeing a bloody played-out gold mine? We don't have the Taj Mahal. We've got the flies and the mossies, mind you. They wouldn't be disappointed there.'

'OK,' replied Delaney, gulping his drink, 'at the other end of town there are those rock formations with the caves and some of the best and oldest Aborigine rock art in the region. It's fenced off right now to keep the yobbos and snoopers away but the experts have been out here to look at it a few times as we all know, and they reckon it's a real beaut site. Unique they tell me. And they reckon some of the paintings are thousands of years old –

maybe some of the oldest in Australia. There's the reservation where the Abos could sell their crafts, though it would mean them moving closer to town.'

There were murmurs of disapproval as he continued 'The railway station could be converted into a visitor centre. Our old Victorian hotel could be updated and extended, if we can get them interested. And there's over a century's worth of mining equipment out there as well as the newer stuff. Oh, and there's that old locomotive a mile or two up the track. I'd say we've enough for an outdoor museum. I already figured out a name for it – *The Museum of Outback Enterprise*. How's that sound?'

'Nice idea, Bill,' said Joe Manson, drawing on his cigarette, 'but you'd need to fence in the Abos to stop some of 'em going walkabout – the older ones at any rate – and you'd need to keep their kids away from the bloody grog when the tourists were around. And I mean *well* away!'

More laughter and Bill Delaney, placing hands on his glass, nodded, 'Yeah – suppose so.'

'Why not leave the Abos where they are?' suggested a woman in a white broad-brimmed hat. 'If someone could get the train running again we could take the tourists to the reservation then deeper into the bush for half-day excursions – with a bar on board, of course.'

Her suggestion, the latter part in particular, met with general approval, but Bill Delaney said, 'I don't know if anyone would finance it. That old engine hasn't worked for so long I reckon she might be past it. As for the few carriages they had and all those wagons – well, I reckon they got scrapped years ago when the rail company took a hiding. There's still that old carriage they left parked outside as a souvenir, though she looks ready to fall apart.'

'The way this whole town'll be going unless a miracle happens,' somebody remarked.

***

The reptile eye of a setting sun peered over the horizon when, at first no more than a wavering speck in the hazed distance, he walked naked and brightly painted out of the desert. The children saw him first and began to call out. The women pulled their children back then in twos and threes the men began to gather. They watched the stranger draw closer but did not move to greet him. Apari knew this was the one he had waited for and the men stood around in a silence broken only by the cries of younger children and the buzz of cicadas in the spreading dusk.

The stranger spoke to no one; looked at no one as he walked slowly but purposefully by, spear in hand, to where the stranded engine waited. His presence was felt like the approach of a storm. Even the most rebellious of the young men somehow knew they ought not to raise their voices or cause a disturbance in his presence.

For a time he stood motionless, gazing only at the locomotive. In fading light he raised his arms to point with spear and hand at the iron bulk. He began to dance – a stamping, shuffling dance that moved him no more than a step or so from where he had first stood. As twilight deepened, their fire cast his wavering shadow upon the engine, darker than the darkness of the iron beast itself and now he was chanting in a low voice. Apari and his people watched and listened but still they moved no closer. From time to time the man's voice rose higher, though they could not understand his words. His shadow, thrown larger by the fire in its final blazing up, grew until it encompassed the locomotive. With the cloak of night drawn over the land he continued to chant, his voice circling as birds in the air. Some of the younger boys at last began to chatter among themselves. Fearing they might shout or throw stones at the man to make him turn and face them, the women ushered them away.

The fire had died to a smouldering glow and stars shone above when the chanting stopped. The stranger stood once more in silence, his form becoming indistinct, then invisible against the bulk of the old engine. Apari's people waited in darkness, listening. For a long time they waited. At last, Apari stepped cautiously forward, intending to ask the stranger what was to happen next.

The spirit man was no longer there.

***

The onlookers had departed when, in the secret depths of the night, there were sounds. Within the dark hulk metal shifted and ground against metal. Something click-click-clicked. Through the ash-strewn firebox, through the clustered tubes of the boiler – a long sigh.

In the cooler air of morning they gathered about and wondered. The stranger had told them nothing. Had imparted no message to Apari. The locomotive stood as it had stood the day before. As it had stood for uncounted days before that.

Later that day a group of Apari's people left the reservation with spear and boomerang to go north where they would meet with members of other tribes far from any town. There they would sing, dance and jigsaw-fit their myths to create the greater picture. Some of those remaining, mainly the young, had no wish to go. They had lost the will. They dismissed the reasons why they should go walkabout. They would prefer to go to the town where they would buy their beer at the bottle shop or general store and their burgers at the take-away before meandering back. If later there was any fighting, if there was too much violence, the police would be there to investigate.

In the following night, more sounds. Scraping. Rattling. The metal beast creaked, grated, shuddered. Voices whispered. Now a cryptic murmuring and a scampering through metal innards. Coupling and connecting rods, driving wheels and brake rigging tensed, strained and shifted. Spiders and lizards fled their haven of repose. A snake dropped from beneath the engine and slithered into the night. Then more voices. Needles quivered nervously behind the grimed glass of gauges. Levers twitched then shook until loose enough to move. Accumulated grit and sand fell as a gentle rain from under the dark form.

***

Something had happened. Apari gazed at the great engine in the morning light. Yes, something had changed, yet there was nothing he could see that appeared any different than on the previous day or in the days before that. But something had happened – was happening. Of that he was certain.

Toward midday a number of the younger men and girls set off to the town. By late afternoon they had returned. By the evening there was drunken fighting and the police were called once more. There were two arrests but the boys would be freed after a day or two of harmless detention.

Apari should have gone walkabout with those of the older men and women who had already left, but he needed to stay because the spirit man's visit had a purpose.

***

On the third evening after the spirit man had left, Apari lay on his makeshift patio bed. He would not sleep inside the house. He never had. That would be an admission of defeat, an abrogation of timeless beliefs, a severing of his ancestral ties. And though the night was placid and warm there was a tension in the air that caused him to listen keenly. There were vague sounds. Murmuring voices. He turned over and looked out through the patio rails. In the obscurity of the night he felt something was happening. He got up from his bed and walked toward the dark and ominous bulk of the locomotive.

Within the dark form life had arisen. A screech of metal cut the air and Apari staggered back. A serpent hiss then a deep growl resonated through the iron cadaver. A dim light shimmered within the cab. A light that grew brighter as he watched. Apari stood wide-eyed, not thinking to look over his shoulder and see if others had been disturbed by the noises. But they had and were hurrying to join him. Clanging metal and the glow within the beast intensified. Within the great metal husk, cryptic voices chanted. The locomotive stirred, shuddered, breathed white vapours, coughed spark-speckled smoke.

Apari could smell the smoke and the burning. He could see flames dance within the firebox to light up the empty cab. The glow dappled his face and naked body ghostly red. He could feel the growing heat yet remained where he was, hands raised in awe as smoke swirled all about to obscure the stars above. A metallic sigh, then another, louder. A shriek of tortured metal. The locomotive wheezed, shuddered - then began to move. Amidst a cacophony of clanging, a monstrous gasp arose followed by an eruption of rolling smoke and steam. The iron beast growled slowly forward, connecting and coupling rods thrust by asthmatic pistons, wheels turning. Smoke and flames engulfed as if to devour the great engine and from their midst emerged the deafening turmoil of its own innards. But it drove on, gaining speed, a bellowing, smoke-venting turmoil of conflagration that soon was thundering along the track as an infernal host in the night.

***

It was the last day of the week and the bar was busy. The blond girl's voice sounded from behind the bar. 'You folks had enough for one evening? I'd like to close in ten minutes.'

Today her eyelashes were longer, her earrings flashing, her dress cut lower, shorter and tighter than usual. It was, after all, Friday. Music blared from two speakers at the far side of the room, submerging the words of several women who sat away from the men in laughter-punctuated conversation.

'Nar,' answered Joe Manson. 'We've only got weekend shifts tomorrow. Might as well make the most of it. I could sink another beer.' He turned to a colleague. 'You care for another, Johnno?'

'Don't think I'll bother, mate,' came John's reply. 'Got to be up early. I'm off to the big smoke first thing. Going to grab myself a slice of civilisation.'

'He means up before nine o'clock,' grinned the blue-frocked woman sitting at a nearby table.

'Bloody hell,' responded John, 'I've been workin' me arse off all day. Give us a break!'

'I'll join you, Joe!' called a man standing at the bar. 'Same again?'

'Sure, Warren. Grab us a couple each. It'll give our lovely Tracey a chance to clear up.'

John pushed aside his empty glass and, getting up, strolled over to the window. Music and conversation filled the smoke-laden air as Tracey pulled the last round of drinks. Her revealing dress prompted another spate of innuendo from those men close to the bar. She considered it no bad thing. In a town where men outnumbered women two-to-one she could take advantage of the competition. She could pick and choose. Until, that was, she could leave the town for ever.

'You blokes need taking in hand,' she quipped.

'Too bloody right we do!' came the inevitable response from one.

'Whenever you're ready, sweetheart,' added another, pretending to loosen his trouser belt.

By the window, John continued to stare.

A cluster of brimming glasses in his hands, the smiling Warren made his way over to the table.

'Hey!' came a shout from across the room. John's voice was all but drowned by the music. 'Hey, everyone!' he called louder, 'there's a fire out there! Something's going on!'

'A fire out where?' someone queried. 'What kind of fire, Johnno?'

Tracey turned down the music and peered across the room.

'How the bloody hell should I know!' answered John. 'It's a big fire from the looks of it!'

'Could be the Abos have set fire to their shacks,' put in someone else. 'Wouldn't be the first time I reckon!'

'That's no bloody house fire!' responded John. 'It's growing too quick! I'll take a look outside!' He strode to the door, pulled it open and disappeared but was back within seconds, his face a mask of wide-eyed panic. 'Everybody get out!' he yelled. 'Out of the bloody place! Get out now!'

Conversation ceased. Above the noise of the music the rumbling grew. On the side of the room opposite the window a lurid shimmering glow had appeared.

***

Apari had watched flames and smoke diminish into the night and only now became aware of others gathered around him in perplexed silence.

Far away a glow pierced the night. A ball of fire erupted lazily skyward to pick out the diminishing line of the railway track. Then came rolling thunder.

Accident

It had been a good day. The meeting had gone well. I was feeling satisfied with myself and I wasn't concerned any more. Well, not so the way I had been when I first set out. I'd had my way in the end because I'd got the deal I wanted. Well someone had to - just as someone had to lose out. Someone always has to lose out, don't they? It's the way things are. That's life.

The weather was overcast and drizzly; not raining enough to keep the windscreen clear but enough to keep it messed up, so I had to keep the washers busy. I recall turning up the radio and listening to music. I don't remember what the music was; I just remember someone playing a saxophone. The notes went on and on, sustained, rising higher and higher. The road was busy and there was a truck. I remember the truck, especially the wheels and how they hissed on the wet road like a waterfall, getting louder, all the time louder. Now roaring. The truck was passing me slowly and the rushing water sound and high-pitched whine from its damned engine were drowning out my radio. I reached out to turn up the sound so I could hear the music.

I don't really know what happened. There was something close to my window, blotting out the light. Then a jolt. Everything shook, including me. Shook every bone in my body.

I started to spin – slowly at first. For a few moments the world outside moved like a merry-go-round. My foot was hard on the brake but I went on spinning, not slow now but quicker. Ever quicker.

Everything was turning, flashing by, becoming a senseless blur so I could no longer hold on to reality. I told myself it was only a dream and that I was in that state when you're passing through the door into real, tactile world, yet part of you wants to remain where it is in the dream because you got to like it that way. But I didn't want to remain where I was because I didn't like it. And the radio was still on, and the music, the saxophone, getting louder, always louder, screaming at me. Or were they my own screams as lights flashed past my eyes and I threw my hands up across my face.

Then it all stopped. There was no longer any sound. The music, the lights - everything. Gone.

***

There was a stillness like I hung in some kind of blind limbo. Then there were sounds again - sounds I couldn't at first understand. I didn't want to open my eyes. I don't quite know why. I stayed as I was, listening to my own breathing and my own heartbeat. After a time I realised what the sound was. Flowing water. I felt warmth on my face. A gentle warmth. Through closed eyes I became aware of red light and I knew it was sunlight shining through my eyelids. I couldn't say how long I remained motionless because this new reality seemed to have no beginning. I might have been floating. Maybe I was in a boat on a river. I was on something quite hard but leaning back against softness. Slowly, very slowly at first, I raised my arms until my fingertips touched my chin and my cheeks. I ran fingers about my face and my eyes, listening to flowing water. And now I could hear birds singing.

Then a voice to my right. 'Come on Charlie, we can't stay here all day!'

It was like the voice of a memory, like someone calling me out of a dream. I opened my eyes, dazzled at first by the sun. She was only a couple of steps away, peering down at me with wide dark eyes. She was smiling. It wasn't a broad welcoming smile – no. It was more a smile of understanding. The kind of smile you offer someone when you're concerned for their well-being. Her hair, the colour of ripening wheat, swept back from a round, thoughtful face and hung down almost to her waist. Was she beautiful? Yes, in an elusive kind of way, she was. Very beautiful.

I just stared. I didn't know what to say. I didn't know who she was. Her expression, though, made it pretty certain she knew me.

'Come on Charlie.' She stepped back with arms folded, waiting for me to get up.

For some time I wondered if it might still be a dream. Then I no longer believed it could be. Water flowed by, shimmering in the sun. There was a breeze on my cheek and I could smell the grass I was leaning against. The possibilities were limited so I considered them. All three of them. Maybe I was insane. Maybe I was suffering from amnesia. Or maybe I was dead. If I was insane I wouldn't know it, so that didn't matter. But I didn't believe I was insane. I didn't believe the third option either. All my senses told me it couldn't be true unless death was just another kind of life. But I didn't believe in life after death. I never had. So I settled for amnesia.

I pushed my hands against soft grass and eased myself up. The fact that I was still wearing my business suit and tie puzzled me, but not as much as her presence. She knew me, so I figured I must know her. Perhaps given enough time things might fall into place and I'd understand what the hell was going on and what I was doing there.

She turned away, looked at me from over her shoulder and began to walk. I followed, watching her tread with casual ease along the riverbank as though she walked it often.

Maybe she did walk it often. Maybe we both did.

She began to pull ahead but I didn't want to hurry because I didn't know where we - where I - was going. There was no mistaking her though - she knew exactly where we were going and she moved along purposeful and confident. I studied the way she was dressed. She wore a plain, long cotton dress. It could have been from any place, any time. But it showed the contours of her body. Lithe and slim, young and active.

I wasn't going to keep up with her; like hell I wasn't. If I fell back, if I gave myself time to think, perhaps all this might begin to make sense. Perhaps things might start falling into place. Perhaps I'd start to understand what I was doing here and where we were heading. But I knew perfectly well who *I* was. I was – I am - Charlie Blackmoor. Charlie Blackmoor - or just plain Charlie.

But she also knew that.

I was deep in thought when she stopped and turned. I'd almost caught up to her when I stopped, too, and we were almost face to face.

'Charlie,' she said, 'we haven't got all day!'

Her expression hinted at a smile though the tone of her voice was urgent.

'Why?' I asked. 'Why are we in a hurry? Why haven't we got all day?'

'Charlie, please,' she answered, 'we can't wait here. We have to keep going.'

'I don't know about that,' I said. 'I like it here. It's quiet and it's pleasant. It's somewhere I could stay a while longer. Yes, maybe I will.'

'No, Charlie!'

'Don't say no. It's good by the river. If we sit down, here, right here, I could think about things. Yes, that's what I want to do - just sit and think for a time. What will a few minutes - what will half an hour matter?' By now I really needed to think and think hard. It occurred to me I could call someone. Someone familiar, just to check if the world was real. I tapped my pockets, I fished around, but there was no mobile phone. Maybe it was still in my car – wherever my car was.

'Charlie, it's getting late. Maybe next time, Charlie. Maybe next time.'

I thought she was going to take hold of my hand. She stepped forward and reached out. But she didn't touch me - just held her hand poised for a moment then let it fall back to her side. Her eyes seemed to see only me. Not the river. Not the trees. Not the sky. Only me.

'Late for what?' I asked. The sun was still quite high.

She looked at me reproachfully. Her gaze sharpened, her lips parted but she didn't speak.

'Late for what?' I repeated. 'Tell me. Just remind me what we're late for. I've forgotten! Don't you see that? It happens to everybody doesn't it? You make appointments, you say you'll do something, and you forget! Well?'

She continued to fix me with those deep pool eyes. When she spoke, I thought she was verging on anger. 'Charlie, this is important. You must understand. You must follow me.'

I'll swear I saw tears in the corners of her eyes. I might not have known where the hell I was going, but she made me feel as though I was denying her everything she ever asked for. And for what? For the sake of a walk along a pathway next to a river that, like my memory, came from nowhere and might have well been going nowhere. What did it matter? If I didn't know where she was taking me, should I care? Maybe it was for the best. Maybe things would be clearer when we got around the next bend. Maybe I'd recognise a bridge, a building, the lay of the land. Something. Anything!

She seemed to read what was going on in my head. As I relaxed, she turned and carried on along the path as before. I followed but the path didn't stay with the river. It moved away into woodland. Soon it narrowed to a little used track. After a minute or so the trees became taller and thicker, the bushes closer. Further along still, they cut out the sun until I only caught glimpses where it daubed fingerprints of light amongst tangled roots and rotting leaves.

Everything felt different. Damp and decay hung heavy in air that had become utterly still. The sound of the river was gone and apart from our footsteps treading the winding pathway, I knew this place was silent. Utterly silent. Before long even the dapples of light had vanished. All I knew was her walking a few paces ahead of me, and the swish of dry, dead leaves. The path, too, was hardly more than a vague track. When I looked beyond her, I couldn't see any track at all. Just the dark forest. That's all there was ahead. Trees, tall and straight, rose up and surrounded us like the piers and columns of some long abandoned cathedral. I didn't like it. Not one bit I didn't!

'Hey!' I called. 'Stop a minute!'

She ignored me and kept on.

'Hey - stop! Just stop! OK?'

Still she went on.

I hesitated. Was I going to leave her and go back to where I was? No, I couldn't do that because I'd be alone and none the wiser. She had the answer. She knew! 'Hey!' I called again. 'Look, just wait! Just wait!'

I knew she'd heard me when she slowed and turned her head. Her voice drifted back. 'Hurry, Charlie – we'll soon be there!'

I began to hurry. In a few moments I'd catch up and I was going to make her stand right there in front of me. Right there until she told me who she was and what was happening! Right there until she told me *everything* I had to know!

Soon I was at her side. 'You have to talk to me because I don't know what's going on! You have to -!'

She ignored me, stared straight ahead and looked about to carry on, so I reached out to grab

her arm. Then I snatched back my hand. 'Oh, Christ
- you're -! What is this? What -?'

Her flesh was cold as ice.

At last she turned but now I didn't want her to.
I backed away. I was scared like I was never scared
before.

'Charlie!' she called. It wasn't a real call, not
the way she'd spoken before. It was a whisper. A
whisper that filled the forest, spread through the
trees and through me. I don't know how long I
stood with her staring back at me but I do know
who made the first move. She did. She reached out
to touch me and I knew I knew I mustn't let her!

I'd always prided myself on never running
away. No, not from anything. I regarded people who
ran away from things as lacking guts no matter what
they had to face. None of that mattered any more. I
turned and I ran like I never ran before. And when
you run, you get more scared still. Or so I found
out.

I heard her behind me. Heard her feet scattering
the leaves so I didn't have to look over my shoulder
to know how close she was. I ran harder and her
voice came again, 'Charlie!' It was still a whisper
but harsh, grating, insistent. It seemed to brush past,
to hover like it wanted to hold me back. I ran harder
until I saw I was on the track and heading the way
I'd come. Ahead, small luminous bursts showed
where the sun was striking through foliage. Beyond
it, I'd be on the real path again and clear of the dark
forest. Fear had taken complete hold on me. A fear
unlike any I'd ever imagined!

'Charlie!' The voice hissed about me like a
whirlwind, danced from side to side then in front.

She was getting closer! Even if she hadn't spoken, I'd have known, I'd have sensed it. The hairs on the back of my neck prickled. My spine buzzed like a power cable.

'Charlie!' It came again, urgent, closer still. I was thrashing my way through the bushes and into the sunlight. I had to keep moving. I dared not falter though my breath came in frantic gasps and my heart pounded hard!

I was getting nearer the river. I could hear the water and smell the grass again. I couldn't hear her footsteps anymore but she was there. I knew she was. Very close. I had to keep on, no matter what. There was the river. I mustn't slow down. Never slow down!

'Charlie!'

It wasn't a whisper, oh, no! No one ever sounded like that. It was a growl. A growl of malice – no, worse. I was by river with my lungs close to bursting. I careered onward until I saw ahead the spot where I had sat. The spot where I had first seen her.

Something touched my shoulder. 'Charlie!'

It was a harsh, discordant shriek - the shriek of some furious and demented thing. I felt coils of air like talons stroking my neck. I cried out as I sped on for I knew that it would any moment take me over and bring me down in a turmoil of horror and despair!

My foot caught something – a root maybe - then I lost my balance and stumbled. I knew she – it was almost on me and I saw it before I came crashing down. I saw the shadow cast ahead of me - the shadow of what she had been. I hit the ground and rolled with the momentum of the fall. Everything spun around, the sun, the trees. Something big and grey, something dreadful beyond words hovered above me. There were red eyes, lights maybe. Faster I seemed to spin until everything became a meaningless blur of flashing colours.

***

The lights were still flashing when I heard my name again. 'Charlie.'

The voice was calm, a voice of understanding. I opened my eyes. There were other voices, people moving about. There were more lights but lights I knew. Flashing lights in blue and red but I didn't understand why. And there was cold drizzle on my face.

'Charlie, you're going to be OK,' she smiled over me. She was adjusting something under my head - something soft. I could see the grey sky above, but I was lying in a shadow. The shadow of a vehicle. It was where the flashing lights came from. Not my car. With my head propped up a little, I could see my car by the crash barrier but it didn't look like my car anymore. My car had been new, clean and unblemished. Not the twisted wreck turned onto its side over there.

Around me were people in uniforms. Some of them busy. Some waiting around. Some of them looking at me. I wanted to get up and go to my car, to look inside and find my things.

'Don't try to move, Charlie,' came her voice.

'Is it bad?' I asked, surprised at how difficult it was to speak those few words

65

'No,' she smiled, closing up a small case that lay at my side.

'You've lost some blood but you'll mend. We got to you just in time.'

'OK to lift him?' came a voice close by.

'She looked up. 'Yes we're all right to move him now.'

They took hold of the stretcher and I began to rise, swinging around toward the open doors of the ambulance. Everyone was looking at me. Me - I was star of the show. There were the usual onlookers who always stopped out of curiosity. People who maybe felt better if they saw the distress of somebody else and thought, 'If it's him then it can't possibly be me.' Then I guess the road was blocked so they couldn't go anywhere. We waited a short while at the open doors. I stared at the people who were staring so hard at me. I was going to smile at them, make some kind of remark. I was going to say, 'Hard luck, maybe you'll see me dead next time around.'

I said nothing. I knew one of those faces. Straight away I knew.

Most of the expressions were pretty bland. But this one was not. She stood a little aside from the rest, motionless, with arms folded, still wearing the cotton dress in spite of the cold, damp air. Those eyes stared hard at me, reproachful, vengeful. Not just at me but into me - into my deepest thoughts. Her lips moved and I could hear her voice, her whisper. I could hear it as I'd heard it by the river bank. 'Next time, Charlie. Next time.'

I had been in a state of shock, of course - they explained that afterwards. They explained how the mind can be affected by the kind of thing that had happened to me. Well, I'm all right now but the memory hasn't gone away. It never will. They said talking about it would help. It didn't. It still doesn't.

Sometimes in broad daylight, even in crowded places, I find myself looking at faces that seem half familiar. I often glance over my shoulder, even in the middle of a conversation. Sometimes people remark on it. They ask if I'm expecting a visitor. I just smile.

Night-time is worse. At night, even in the summer, even when there are plenty of people about, I never walk out anywhere without company. Never. And when I'm alone in the dark her words return as if she waits close by, 'Next time, Charlie. Next time.'

Canyon

A new star appeared in the morning heavens, bright above a soft haze of mists that hung in shifting veils above the canyon floor. The star grew. It drifted westward against an apricot sky, delicate counterpoint to a harsh, newly risen sun that furrowed the hand of day across buttressed walls of burning red. The star grew. Resolving itself as not a star but an engine of fire, poised, descending into a realm of frigid desolation. It slowed, dizzyingly high, but already fallen below a soaring immensity of cliffs, a glowing mote against the curtained backdrop of a surreal stage.

The shuttle slowed further, hovered, blasted smoke and sand aside with a thunder that echoed across the wide valley to violate a kingdom of silence that had brooded unmeasured ages. The fires died and silence stole back to reclaim its realm. The shuttle rested, sunlight gleaming on her hull. About her, ghostly spirals persisted for a time before drifting to oblivion.

***

'We're down safely and all checks completed,' said the smiling Leonid, eyes darting across instrument panels and monitors. 'Here in this place before any of them. Here before the Europeans, the Asians, even before the damned Americans!'

'They've been playing it carefully - all of them,' remarked Vasili. 'Heading for the wide open spaces and uplands.'

'Well, I say caution is no bad thing,' responded Nikolai. 'We're a long way from home, even with Andrei orbiting in the mother ship and the

Americans with their base established near Olympus. Apart from that, our people never did a ground scan of this area. Always trying to save expense. It would be different if they came here themselves.'

Leonid turned to the main viewplate and began scanning the valley. 'Never mind, Nikolai - here we are, Candor Chasm, or at least a small part of it. One of the most spectacular places on Mars. Look at those cliffs; they rise over five kilometres above us. Fantastic!'

'Do they look that high to you?' said Nikolai. 'I wouldn't care to try and guess from here. Something on that scale - it's almost impossible to figure out even from this close.'

'Close?' smiled Leonid, 'We're over eight kilometres away. If it wasn't for the scree and the boulders, I would have brought us down much closer.'

'Well I am glad you didn't,' said Nikolai, staring out at vast cliffs, ablaze now with sunlight. 'Nobody can be sure how long ago those landslides took place. Who knows - the sound of our engines might have brought the whole lot down upon us. It happens on Earth - avalanches, rock falls. It only takes a shout and down it all comes.'

'Well, none of it will reach us here,' observed Vasili, 'This part of the canyon is flat as water. I can see nothing nearby larger than a pebble. When do I go outside, commander?'

'Ah, yes,' replied Leonid, 'you won the draw to be first on the ground, did you not.'

'How could we forget,' breathed Nikolai, staring at the viewplate.

Vasili ignored the remark. It was not the first and he did not expect it would be the last. Why Nikolai had taken a dislike to him Vasili could not say. For some minutes they were silent, checking instruments and readings. Vasili munched conspicuously on a chocolate bar so as to be first to eat anything in the canyon - much to the barely suppressed annoyance of Nikolai.

'We're scheduled to remain here six days before re-joining Andrei in orbit,' said the commander, rubbing his hand across a stubbled chin, 'but I don't see why -'

'What was that?' interrupted Nikolai.

Leonid looked from one to the other. 'What was what? I didn't hear anything.'

'No, not hear - feel!' responded Nikolai. 'Didn't you feel it? Didn't you feel the ship move?'

'There was a slight shudder,' said Vasili, 'nothing more. The ship is settling into the sand a little. Our readings from orbit showed the ground was not be well compacted.'

The commander eyed Nikolai. 'You're getting jumpy, I think. We've travelled millions of kilometres through empty space and now we're safely on the ground, you're getting jumpy.'

Nikolai relaxed. 'Maybe I've been cooped up for too long. It didn't seem to matter so much when we left Earth.'

'Then you go out there first instead of me,' offered Vasili, 'I really wouldn't care. It's not as if we're the first people to set foot on Mars - though I wouldn't have minded.'

Nikolai considered the offer. 'No, Vasili, it's really not that important. You get on with it. What's another few hours after all these months.'

'As I was about to say,' continued the commander, 'Vasili can get suited up as soon as he wishes. No more than an hour outside though, Vasili - OK? There's work to be done so there is no reason why you shouldn't put down a few instruments and collect the necessary samples whilst you're about it. Nikolai can take a stroll in a different direction afterwards. Maybe I'll wait until the afternoon.' His eye fell upon the environmental readout panel. 'And don't be fooled by the bright sun, Vasili. It's minus sixty-two Celsius out there at present!'

'Ha - maybe,' smiled Vasili, 'but that is not much colder than the winters where I used to live and we didn't grow up with the luxury of heated space suits!'

***

Vasili waited for the outer door to open. In his suit pocket was the photograph he had brought on the long journey. The photograph of her. Perhaps this was the first time anyone had taken such a photograph with them when venturing out on this harsh and forbidding world.

The door slid aside and without thinking, Vasili breathed in deeply, as though tasting the scents of a spring morning on Earth. Stark sun glared from his visor and his gaze fell upon the surrounding escarpment, rising sharp and clear in tenuous, unbreathable air. High above, along the upper rim he observed great concave recesses - each a giant bite several kilometres long, where the land above had collapsed to slide like splaying fingers into the valley.

Swinging about, he gripped the metal ladder and began a measured descent. Two thirds of the way down, something happened. He stopped, looked up at the ship. The ladder had shifted. He was quite certain it had shifted. Perhaps it was his weight. Vasili continued his descent and, almost at the bottom, peered down at the base of the ladder. Yes, it had moved. In the sand, where it had initially rested, there were furrows. The ladder had slid toward the ship by some thirty centimetres.

'Vasili, is everything OK out there?' came the voice of Leonid. 'We felt another tremor - the ship is still settling.'

'Oh, yes - I'm just about to - there! I've taken my first step on Mars! Well - I can't say it feels so very different than Earth.'

'Fine, we'll keep you on screen from now on. I'll transmit your historic first walk back to Andrei later.'

'Why not now, then Andrei can relay it straight to Earth? They will see me on television and -.'

'You should know why, Vasili,' interrupted Leonid, 'Andrei has moved into a higher orbit for survey work. He'll be out of contact for the next ten hours.'

Vasili stepped away from the ladder, testing the lower gravity of this strange, breath-taking place. He stopped, gazed about, then trudged on through powder-fine sand until he was some sixty metres from the ship. To the west, immense curtains and vast terraces were awash with light. To the other side of the canyon, sunlight had caught only the rim.

But it glowed red. Glowed as though molten lava spilled over the edge, streaked here and there with vivid ochre.

'Hey, what a sight this is!' he called over the radio. 'I've walked through simulations - I thought I knew how it would all be. But this -!'

'Keep on relaying it, Vasili, whilst you have the chance,' came Leonid's voice. 'It's a good time of the day with the sun still low.'

'OK,' replied Vasili, checking his suit cameras as he strode on. 'I'll relay some of those landslips - and that stone pillar over there - hell - my sensor gives it a height of nearly two kilometres! Something like that could never stand on Earth. It's weight would bring it crashing down. Maybe I'll take a closer look. Maybe I can do that and be back in an hour.'

'Don't go too close, Vasili! Our landing might have shaken parts of it loose. We have it on screen and there seems to be - Oh! Something's happening - we -! Oh - what -!'

Vasili turned to look back along the trail of his own footprints, not understanding for a moment what his eyes beheld. The ship was moving! Yes, she was twisting about! Tilting over to one side!

'Commander! What's happening? What's -?'

Over his radio came incoherent shouting. Then sounds of panic. Vasili started back - striding through fine sand that kicked up in clouds and dragged at his boots to hamper progress. Then he stopped. Stopped and began to comprehend the true horror. The shuttle was sinking! Already her ground stabilisers had disappeared and the twisted metal ladder swung out at a crazy angle. Vasili trudged on, calling over his radio, within his helmet an incomprehensible babble. Voices of desperation. Angry thunder reached his ears and the ship trembled. Trembled then began to fall through the sand. Vasili watched the canyon floor give way beneath her. Watched sand pour into a draining well. He called out, struggled on with arms outstretched but the ship foundered as though engulfed by a tempestuous sea. Someone cried out then with a roar, with a screech of tortured metal, she vanished below the surface whilst torrents of sand rushed inward to consume her. Vasili, carried along with the flow, started backwards. The ground ahead was now a broad depression and he was caught as an ant in a sand spider's trap. He fell and began to slither, all the time calling out in helpless rage, expecting to be swallowed up and for the world to darken. Expecting that which he most dreaded - to be buried alive.

The sand slowed. Vasili lay face down, arms and legs outstretched, his visor blanked out. There was now stillness but Vasili did not move.

At last he turned his head to stare across the slope of a shallow sand-bowl. Of the shuttle there was nothing to be seen. Vasili remained where he was because he no longer believed this could be real. The ground gave a gentle tremor. Before his eyes a fountain of sand burst upwards with a loud hiss several metres above the centre of the bowl. A plume of white vapour arose beneath this to spread lazily in the thin air. The ship had ruptured. Air, and life, had departed from her.

He continued to gaze at the spot where they had landed. Perhaps this was a bad dream - a creation of a mind stressed after the long voyage. Soon the nightmare would release him. Perhaps if he looked away then back again, the ship would be there and his commander would ask why he was sitting idly in the sand, daydreaming when there was work to be done.

Vasili struggled to his feet, sand pouring from his limbs. He gazed along the canyon then turned about. There was no ship.

As he scrambled clear of the bowl and onto level ground another shocking reality bore upon him. He was alone in a lifeless vastness. Alone and as far from help as anyone could be. He had experienced isolation before. In the frozen wastes of his homeland he had often been alone. But that had been by choice and remote as it was, there had always been someone he could converse with - no matter how far away they might be. In this spectacular, utterly hostile landscape, under shimmering, golden heavens, there was no one with whom he could communicate.

Above the canyon rim, Vasili observed thin ribbons of ice crystal. Ghostly streamers glowing high in the sky. He knew of no satellite able to relay his calls for help. The nearest human life was the American base south-east of Mount Olympus. They had passed high above the great volcano in orbit, talked and laughed with the Americans. It seemed at the time they were not so far away. But now -. It mattered little that he could not calculate the exact distance to the American station. Between the canyon and Olympus was a landscape of rising, cratered desert for at least another three thousand kilometres. There also reared the volcanic immensity of Ascraeus to bar the way. Even to consider such a journey would be entirely pointless. Apart from that there were the great walls of the canyon. There could be no way up those walls.

Tuning through the radio frequencies, he wondered if there might after all be a satellite able to respond. Maybe another ship in orbit. Someone! Who could say what the other powers on Earth were doing? They did not readily declare their intentions. Vasili tried again and again. He listened long and hard. There was nothing.

There was Andrei, of course! Andrei would be overhead in less than ten hours. Andrei could call the Americans. They had a supply ship in orbit - and their ground vehicle. They would come for him. It might take a day – maybe longer. But they could do it. They must do it!

A day? Ten hours? Vasili would not have ten hours of power and air in his life support pack. His was only intended as a short excursion. On checking the read-out, he saw, and he knew. There was enough power for little more than three hours. He set about to analyse the situation. Examined his circumstance from every angle, yet every thread weaved back to one truth. A truth that grew until its grim shadow blotted out the guttering flame of hope. A truth soaring high in his thoughts as the monolith that towered skyward from the canyon floor. Vasili would never leave the canyon alive.

Across the valley, a wind had started to blow. His suit microphones picked up its sighing whisper and he watched streamers of sand flow as a ghostly incoming tide just above the ground. The shallow depression marking the tomb of his companions would soon be indistinguishable from the rest of the canyon floor. His own footprints would likewise be no more.

He gazed along the canyon until his attention fell once more upon the monolith and he wondered how things might end. It would, he considered, have been better to have perished with Leonid and Nikolai. At least his life would have ended quickly. What were these last hours worth to him? Perhaps he should finish it right now. It would be easy to do that. So very easy.

Vasili had no wish to end his life.

He set off in the direction he had taken before the disaster. Toward the great sandstone pillar. He asked himself why he was doing that, but the answer was simple. The pillar was more than a monument – more than a spectacular landmark. It was a goal to be attained. The only thing that had meaning in a life soon to end. Maybe others would be attracted to it and find him when they came here to discover what had befallen the expedition. If they ever did. Andrei had been out of contact over the horizon when they had made their descent. He should have waited before shifting orbit but time was so important. Anything could have happened as far as Andrei was concerned. How would he know if they had ever have reached the canyon at all?

Vasili arrived back at the point where he had earlier stopped to find his earlier footprints almost obliterated. Any message he might scrape out in the sand would disappear before the day ended. There was no message he could leave, not even his frozen remains. The sand would engulf those as well.

A strange notion beset Vasili. He imagined himself a tiny beetle trapped within some great, deserted hall. Eventually, the beetle would die and fall to the floor, only to dissolve into the dust. As with the fate of the insect, what might happen to him was of no significance at all. The vastness of the canyon and of that stark monolith were the vastness of his despair and of his loneliness. Vasili walked on. Yes, he must reach the great stone pillar, glowing bright in the morning sun. Attaining it would be his final achievement. His monument. Vasili walked but for a while seemed to get no closer to the pillar. Eventually however, the monolith began to grow. Further on and it towered mightily into the sky. Not far to go now. Not far.

At the base of the tower he came upon a chaotic assemblage of boulders and slabs that must have crashed down from its monstrous height - perhaps yesterday, perhaps a million years ago. Vasili found a slab of convenient size and seated himself so that the sun fell upon him and cast his shadow across the side of the monolith.

The wind had abated. The canyon no longer seemed threatening but appeared benign and peaceful. A place of majestic wonder. Vasili studied his surroundings for a while then reached into a utility pocket on his pressure suit from which he withdrew the photograph.

'Ah, Elena,' he breathed gazing at her image. 'Elena, if you could see this place. If only you could.' Vasili arose and stepped forward with arms raised. 'I now claim it as my own. I am lord of this land! King, tsar, emperor - whatever takes my fancy! Above my throne rises a great monument - a symbol of my power as I survey my realms! I claim everything in the canyon as mine even as the canyon claims me!'

Vasili returned to the slab and once again was seated. On the photograph, as in his memory, were her smile and her green eyes and Vasili asked, 'Are you thinking of me now, Elena? Do you see me in your thoughts, so far away on the other side of the sun? Are you thinking of me as I sit in this strange place and think of you?'

Her image and her voice filled his thoughts. Ghosts and whispers. They were together at his hometown in the spring. Together watching streams glitter after the thaw of a long, bitter winter. Together watching the landscape cry out an ecstasy of colour in welcome to a brief and hectic summer. She had been with him on that last day at the spaceport, far to the south of their home. With him the day when he and the others had left Earth on their long voyage through emptiness. Somehow the journey, Andrei, Leonid and Nikolai, seemed less real than those last days on Earth with Elena.

Time flowed by. Vasili was half awake, half dreaming, when the indicator inside his helmet began to flash. The sun was high above and his shadow no longer fell upon the red wall of the pillar but had rotated about to be cast over rubble close by. The life support warning would become more insistent, more urgent. Pulling open the flap of the small control panel on his upper arm, Vasili cancelled the signal.

After a while he arose from the slab and stepped to the base of the pillar. The effort had not been great and he knew the shortness of breath afflicting him had little to do with that. Here was a place free of rubble. A place where the wind had piled sand against the monolith to knee height. Vasili lowered himself to the ground, his backpack resting against solid rock. The sun was full upon him but even so, he was becoming cold. His hand fell a second time to the control box and his finger touched the three red buttons in correct sequence. The gas that filtered into his breathing system was not noxious, not poisonous. It brought only peace. In a while, Vasili was comfortable and regret had given way to contentment. In his hand lay the photograph of Elena. Hers was the last image he wished to see before he closed his eyes.

***

A shadow fell across the motionless form. A shadow soft and amorphous. Then whispers as a sigh of breezes emerging from the secret places of the canyon.

'The being will soon die. We can do nothing. It is alien to us.'

'The minds of its kind have been closed to our own. Perhaps this one will yield.'

'Yes, it may yield. You must try. If you succeed, we may all understand.'

'Wait - I am entering. It offers no resistance. I am seeing - yes, I am seeing but there is much confusion. There is much I do not comprehend.'

'But it begins to yield.'

'Yes, it begins to yield. This mind is opening up to me. Becoming clearer. I am seeing, now. It carries images of its own world. Many images. Wonderful images. They are so strange. There is much water - oceans as once we had. On the surface there is life. Everywhere, life. They have built great structures and there are machines like the machines they bring to our world. So perplexing. But I feel their minds and their desires.'

'We see them through you now,' came other voices. 'Yes we see them but there is one image this being holds - one of its own kind that shines brighter than the others. Do you understand what it means?'

'Yes, I begin to understand. It is a strong image. So strong, so real within the being that if we join together, we can make it ours and the being will understand.'

***

'Vasili.'

Vasili part opened his eyes. 'What - who is it?'

'Vasili, I am here.'

His vision was blurred though it cleared after some seconds. His limbs weighed heavily, he was very cold and he could do little more than raise his head. 'Elena? Elena - I heard your voice.'

'Vasili.'

His eyes widened. 'Elena - what are you -? No! Oh no, it cannot be you! Not here!'

But she was there, kneeling by him, sun-burnished raven hair brushing her cheek, the clear light of the valley glinting in her eyes. His breathing fitful, Vasili summoned the little strength remaining to him, lifted an arm and reached out to touch her. 'Elena - out here - how can you live? How - how can it be you?'

'Do not be afraid, Vasili. I am with you in the canyon.'

'Elena - you will stay? You will stay - with me?'

'I will stay with you, Vasili. You will no longer be alone. See, I hold your hand, I will be by your side whilst you rest and sleep. Sleep now. Tomorrow, we will walk together in the canyon and in the mists. Together, in the sand and the wind. I will never leave you, Vasili. Never.'

Her image filled his vision. His eyes closed. A smile touched his lips. 'Elena.'

***

'The being has ceased, yet the images from its mind are with us. And what images they are.'

'We are saddened. It so wanted to live. Its kind cannot persist beyond the body. We have its memories but the awareness that created them is gone forever. It could never truly share.'

'That is dangerous. If each cannot know what the other knows, how can there be harmony. How can we know what they will do to our world. They themselves cannot know.'

'We must remain unseen. We must watch them. We must see inside them and try to understand. This being has given us the key. We know many others will follow the few we have encountered because it was in the mind of this one.'

'The time may come when we need to protect ourselves from them.'

'Yes we will wait. We will watch and we will wait.'

***

Vasili remained, arm raised, fingers poised to touch that which had never been. Soon, the drifting sands of the canyon would claim him.

82

Rafferty

Rafferty's entry into this world was a quiet affair. There was no flurry of activity as the time drew close, no anxious call to midwife or hospital, no one with medical skills in attendance. His arrival passed unnoticed, the secret of a moonless night. A night with no sound save a mournful owl's cry and the distant barking of a restless dog. No sound other than a half waking sigh of satisfaction in a dark and lonely room.

Quite remarkable, though, was the development of one so new to the world. To have reached full and responsible maturity in so short a time would have been beyond belief had not proof of Rafferty's living and breathing been attested in official documentation. And if official documents maintained it, then Rafferty must somehow exist.

***

Montague stood proudly before the mirrored backdrop of glass shelves, ornamental tankards and brightly illuminated bottles, his face a sleek-haired mask of genial charm. Some might have regarded the ruddy complexion, small but ever-sharp eyes peering from within well-upholstered flesh as a sign of over-indulgence, but no one ever voiced that opinion. Nor did they comment upon his notion of style, despite the slightly over-large fit of an unfashionable check jacket enhanced by a too conspicuous bloom protruding from a wide lapel. At least not they didn't whilst Montague was within earshot.

Montague had been running the Skinner's Arms for over a year and maintained a welcoming and orderly house. Since false references and a talent for bluff had lubricated him into the job, the Skinner's had experienced a marked rise in profits with Montague regarded by many of its customers as the epitome of a good publican. Sited on the corner of a run-down inner suburb street, the Skinner's Arms needed Montague as much as he needed it. Not the most upmarket of venues, it might otherwise have been forced to close. Now it boasted an immense television screen devoted to football and other entertainment scenes devoid of any intellectual value.

In the dimmer hinterland of the bar, most of the tables were occupied though the hour was early. A medley of chatter drifted above the eager souls clustered before the beer pumps. An occasional phone chirp demanded someone's attention. Two assistants - there were usually three in the bar - busied themselves passing drinks and taking cash. From close by the main door drifted the electronic warbling of the eye-bewitching fruit machine, punctuated by the rare, but to Montague unpalatable, clatter of a pay-out.

'Evening Monty!'

'Evening Alan - evening, Joe.' Montague's smile broadened. He unclasped fleshy hands from behind his back to rest upon the counter. 'What'll it be?'

'Two pints of Habsburg please, Monty,' replied one.

'Short staffed tonight are we?' asked the other as Montague eased back the pump to deliver over the first glass.

'Looks that way.' he answered, watching bright amber gush into the second glass. The order was dealt with in time for Montague to note the furtive arrival of his missing member of staff. Stooped in vain hope of passing unseen, the youth sidled through the doorway at the rear of the bar in the process of shedding his jacket. Montague edged toward him, arms rigid by his side, face still wearing an expression of casual amiability. His whisper, close to the ear of the new arrival, fell with a thud of a war drum. 'Where the bloody 'ell you been?'

The barman, a slender, fair-haired lad, saw a less than benign Montague behind the smile. 'Sorry, Mr Powell, I was late home from college today. Exams are coming up and -.'

'Oh - bleedin' exams now is it. Third evening late this month I make it, sunshine. Next time, don't bother to show up at all!' He moved away from the youth, his image of congeniality unsullied. 'Evening Mrs Jenkins! Left him in front of the telly tonight, eh? What'll it be, love?'

***

To the casual observer, Montague kept an evening staff of four on busier nights at bar, kitchen and small restaurant. If things became a little difficult, as now and then they might, Montague was always ready to do his share. And when things became more than a little difficult - well, the customers rarely complained.

The brewery, those faceless people who employed Montague, would not have been so accommodating. The number of staff was officially one more than had ever been encountered at the

Skinner's Arms. Had the brewery seen fit to investigate they would have determined the true recipient of his pay. But Montague's scheme had worked perfectly these past twelve months. He had given name, appearance and personality to his creation. It was a person with no roots; someone who might work a while and then move on. Someone with no permanent address.

Montague had embarked early upon a life of deceit but until his present situation the misdemeanours had been of shorter duration. Assisting on a milk round he had discovered early on how easy it was to charge customers more than they actually owed. Broader landscapes had found him working for a motorcycle dealer where cash jobs in the evening using the firm's materials could earn more than his regular pay. Time spent in the employ of a washing machine service agent proved yet more lucrative. Every machine that occasioned his visit needed a new motor. This it got - reconditioned - from the previous machine that had also needed a new motor. The fact that an electrical short-circuit and resulting house fire had cost three lives was of no concern to him.

'Always grab the opportunity,' had been his philosophy. 'In five minutes it might be gone.' So for Montague, tomorrow had never mattered. Until now.

Montague had begun to desire that which had been absent from his ignoble existence. Status. Status, and with it, respect. His situation vis-à-vis the Skinner's Arms had provided both. It had opened new doors and it had offered the prospect of a secure job in precarious times. Yet opportunities were still opportunities and Montague was still Montague. But the virtual employee's existence might be called into question at any time. Never had Montague so much to lose. A voice from the other side of the bar cut into his thoughts. 'Care for one yourself Monty?'

The place had filled up nicely and the babble was music to his ears.

'Much obliged, Dave! Just a half of mild if that's OK.'

On finishing the drink, Montague sallied forth into ordered clamour, collecting empty glasses, stopping to greet regulars and not so regulars.

'Keep 'em happy,' he often told himself. 'Show a decent profit and nobody will interfere.'

Of late those words carried less conviction. He was threading a route back to the bar with two fistfuls of glasses when he encountered a member of staff in momentary lapse of activity.

'Derek!' he hissed, ensuring only Derek heard. The youth was startled by Montague's grinning-ogre smile. 'There's more to collect over there and there's people at the end waiting to be served. Get a bloody move on!'

The youth obliged, knowing the reputation Montague had for dispensing with any member of staff who did not respond promptly to his demands.

'Not married yet Monty?' asked a middle-aged man close by as Montague set the glasses down on the counter.

'Married, Jim? God no, not me. I'm too busy for that sort of caper. Maybe next week if things ease up a bit!'

Two middle-aged, heavily made up women drinking at a table nearby broke into inane giggles. One of them ogled Montague, 'You've never asked either of us, Monty.'

Montague turned with broadening smile. 'Play your cards right, love, and you could both be in with a chance.'

Facetious his remark may have been but marriage was a subject Montague had begun to consider. He was conscious of those accumulating years that, like geological strata, overlaid the once fresh landscapes of youth. Yet he did have a partner: Rafferty. Rafferty was closer to Montague than anyone had ever been - but that was about to change. That very morning, the decision had been made as Montague, bending over the bathroom sink, regarded the bulbous, watery-eyed image that stared back with grizzled reproach from the shaving mirror. Rafferty was a common enough name in Ireland, and it was to Ireland Montague intended his virtual assistant should return. Naturally, he'd have to take more care over his spending. Rafferty had paid for the hidden extras: expenses that included an occasional mid-week visit to a seaside hotel with one of several lady friends, as well as their meals out in the evening.

But Rafferty had outgrown his original purpose. Montague had lain awake at night considering the other's contribution to the day-to-day running of his petty empire. Some procedures had become attributable to Rafferty, if only on paper. In times of solitude Montague found himself asking Rafferty's opinions when it came to matters he alone should have dealt with. Even in the issue of taking on and dispensing with staff, Rafferty's shade had been consulted. On the other hand, when some detail was left unattended, some item not ordered in time or a delivery not checked, Montague felt it was as much Rafferty's responsibility as his own. Such thoughts loomed large when he stood in the deserted bar after closing time.

Rafferty had become a liability.

During Montague's absences from the Skinner's Arms the senior barman, aided by a little extra cash, took added responsibility. Montague had made it clear his journeys were a painful obligation. The notion of a sick mother at a hospital some distance away had been planted in their minds long ago. And so grave was the lady's situation that even the most discreet of enquiries might upset her caring son. Her death, her second death in effect, would coincide with the demise of Rafferty. Yet with the demise of those extra payments, Montague's grief would be genuine.

In Montague's report to the brewery, the phantom assistant would be found responsible for the disappearance of various items, including bottles of Irish whiskey, a beverage to which Montague himself was partial. Under such circumstances, Rafferty would leave no forwarding address. The dismissal was to take place that coming Friday and a letter – it had to be a printed letter and not an e-mail - sent the following day. There was still, of course, Rafferty's bank account. That could, no - *would* be closed once the report was posted.

The teeth-gritting day of decision arrived and by evening all was made ready. Ascending narrow, creaking stairs to his room at the rear of the building, Montague intended to remove bank card and letter from their hiding place then conceal both in his jacket pocket. He opened the door to his room, not wishing to disturb the quietness within. Here was his refuge from the world of chatter and clatter below: his place of contemplation, of self-knowledge. He stood on the edge of darkness, finger poised upon the light switch.

Something was wrong.

He sensed the air had been disturbed before he entered. It still coiled in secret vortices about dark corners. Montague listened for a time then switched on the light. Nothing appeared out of place. He switched on the radio, removed his jacket and laid it upon the single bed. Kneeling before the chest of drawers by the bed he pulled open the bottom drawer. Hands pushed beneath intimate softness, fingers searched by touch alone. Not finding what he sought, Montague pulled out socks and underwear, placing them aside on the floor until the drawer was empty. He repeated the operation with the drawer above - even reaching behind and beneath the chest. Montague swore under his breath. The letter, chequebook - Rafferty's chequebook - were gone. His brief search throughout the remainder of the room was cursory. Montague knew exactly where both items had been concealed.

Perplexing as the disappearance was, the letter could be rewritten on Saturday morning and the matter of the account sorted out the same day or, if the bank was not amenable, on Monday. The missing items played on his mind through much of that night whilst the image of Rafferty refused to vanish. Its husk, like the nymph shell of a departed insect, still hovered.

***

On Saturday, Montague was too busy to rewrite the letter or to visit the bank. Still, that first weekend without Rafferty passed little differently from any other - except for a minor occurrence.

At closing time that evening and again on Sunday, a slim dark man wearing an old, grey coat and trilby hat, pulled down so as to obscure in shadow the lower part of his face, was amongst the last to leave the bar. Montague might not have noticed him had it not been for the hat. Nowadays unfashionable, hats were seldom worn outside, let alone indoors. On both occasions, the figure had been seated in a dimly lit alcove on the far side of the room - but never observed at the bar.

On Monday morning Montague posted the rewritten letter and called into the bank. It was some distance from the Skinner's Arms and he'd been there only once before - to open the account in Rafferty's name. It was a small, busy bank, the only one still remaining thereabouts, and Montague waited ten impatient minutes before finding himself at the cashier's window. Behind this sat a regulation-tidy youth with alert blue eyes.

'How may I help you, sir?' the youth asked with pre-programmed enthusiasm.

'I want to close my current account, mate,' answered Montague. 'The name's Rafferty. Trouble is I seem to have mislaid the chequebook. Does that matter?'

'Not really, sir,' replied the cashier, 'Chequebooks are now being discontinued. Do you have on-line facilities?'

Montague was taken aback, blurting, 'No – no, mate, I don't.' Montague did possess a computer but did not trust, and had never attempted, to use on-line banking.

'Have you some identification?' followed up the cashier.

From his worn leather wallet Montague tugged the debit card issued in the name of Rafferty.

'Fine,' remarked the youth, turning aside to call up relevant information on his screen. After some finger tapping, he excused himself and left the chair, only to return with an expression of uncertainty. 'Sir,' he announced, laying a printed form out on the other side of the partition, 'you closed your account on the Saturday just gone. We have your signature here.'

Montague scrutinised the document. It was an acknowledgement of closure bearing the name of P. Rafferty, exactly as Montague had signed it when opening the account.

'You drew out five hundred and sixty-eight pounds and twelve pence,' continued the cashier, with a merest hint of accusation. Indecisive seconds pulsed by and the cashier now regarded him with suspicion.

Montague considered that to dispute the matter would be against his interests yet he could not simply turn and walk out. 'Must be losing the old memory,' he breathed, 'I've several accounts around the place. It's - er, not always easy to keep up with everything - right? If I can speak to the person I dealt with on Saturday, it'll help me get sorted out – OK?'

The cashier left his position then emerged into the main hall where he entered a glass-walled office situated at the rear. After a consultation, during which sharp glances were directed at Montague, the cashier returned with a slim, smartly attired girl in her mid-twenties.

'Will you step this way, sir, please?' she said coolly, indicating the office. 'I believe you have a query regarding your closed account, Mr Rafferty.'

'Yes, dear,' Montague answered as they entered, 'I've been shown the signed form but I can't remember coming in and closing it, see. Tell you the truth, love, I'd had a few too many the night before so Saturday's a bit of a fog. Trouble is, I can't find none of the cash. Not like me to lose money!'

She regarded him unsmiling as both sat facing one another. 'I promise you, sir, you did close the account. You handed your chequebook to me and we paid over your cash. You didn't have your debit card just then but that has been cancelled in any case. Yours was in fact the only account closed that day.'

'Remember my face do you, love?' he asked, leaning closer.

'Not really, Mr. Rafferty,' she answered. 'We were extremely busy but I assure you I do recall the transaction and you have seen the record.'

'Silly of me wasn't it, sweetheart,' smiled Montague, rising awkwardly from the chair. 'Senior moment must have turned out a senior day or two.'

Montague left the bank. The money had disappeared and the matter had to rest. Nevertheless, somebody else must know the account had been kept in a bogus name. But who?

***

Montague was not his buoyant self that evening though, being Monday, the customers were fewer in number. From behind the bar, he engaged in small talk with those regulars reluctant to miss out on an evening's drinking.

Later that night he once more became aware of the man in the grey coat. He had not seen him enter but there he was, seated in the same alcove as before. He had before him a half full one-pint glass and, after an hour's intermittent observation, Montague was convinced the glass had not been touched. The visitor seemed not to have moved at all yet Montague felt the man was watching him. Closing time approached when Montague, waiting until one of the barmen had moved around the far end of the counter where he was out of sight from most of the room, strolled casually over to his side. 'Er, George, looks like there's an old bloke gone to sleep in the alcove by the fireplace. Wake 'im up will you and make sure he's all right. Don't want no dead customers clutterin' the place.'

By the time Montague returned to his previous spot the barman was hurrying back with armfuls of empty glasses. Setting these upon the counter he announced, 'Nobody there now Mr. Powell. Must have cleared off home.'

Ten minutes later, the final bell rang.

***

Tuesday was the occasion of someone's birthday. What would have been a moderately busy evening had by eight o'clock become noisy and crowded as a Saturday night. Centre of attraction was a conspicuously overweight middle-aged woman with spiked, peroxide-blond, red-tinged hair, thick spectacles, a loud mouth and over-fleshed thighs squeezed together by a short pink skirt. It was not clear to Montague which of those in her vicinity were part of the retinue but money seemed to be in free supply on this rowdy occasion. Drinks were bought for all present including the bar staff and Montague. Their demands kept him serving and busy in conversation much of that evening.

It was past ten-thirty when, through the gap in the crowd, Montague saw the figure in the grey coat. He no longer doubted the man was watching him. Then the gap closed and the figure was hidden. But from time to time, as people moved to and fro, Montague caught sight of him and imagined he saw light reflected from eyes beneath the brim of the hat. Montague turned as a barman eased past. 'It's OK, Derek, I'll bring 'em in from that side, you do the other.' His next words were an unheard murmur. 'If it's some bleedin' snooper onto me over that bank account I'll find out right now.' Pushing through the crowd he emerged before the alcove only to find seated there a young man and a girl. Both looked up as Montague glanced about, saying, 'Sorry to butt in, mate. Where's the bloke who was sat here just now - the one with the funny 'at on?'

The young man peered back. 'Can't say, we only grabbed the space a second ago.'

Montague forced a smile whilst gathering glasses from the table. One of them was still half full. Leaving it where it stood, he manoeuvred his way back to the bar.

***

After the backslapping, the shrieks, the kisses and goodbyes, after the diminishing clamour, after the bar room stragglers had gone, Montague and the two barmen finished clearing up. With their departure he crossed to the main door and fastened the bolts.

The Skinner's Arms lay silent. Montague stood upon an empty stage with the players gone.

The many small lights cast odd, confusing shadows about empty tables as he continued on, passing back behind the counter then through to the rear where he locked the back doors. He usually climbed the stairs to his room where he would spend an hour reading or watching television before retiring to bed. This evening Montague needed another drink.

Returning to the brightly lit sanctuary of the bar he switched off the main room lights and dispensed a generous measure of Irish. Leaning forward, elbows hard upon the counter, he peered out from the island of light into an obscurity of vague forms. Strange how different the place felt. Alien and forsaken in its emptiness.

The creak of a chair sounded from the far side of the room. A shadow moved. Someone was there. Montague let his glass slip to the counter, spattering some of its contents. In the alcove by the fireplace he could make out a dark figure in grey coat and a trilby hat.

'What the 'ell!' Montague exclaimed. 'Who're you? How d'you get back in 'ere?'

There was no reply.

Montague waited charged seconds. At last he started to the end of the counter, pushed through the opening and moved into semi-darkness. Half way across the room he faltered. 'All right! Who the 'ell are you? Speak or I call the coppers!'

The figure stirred, arose as drifting smoke, lifted its head, gazed upon Montague with eyes dark and empty. Montague stepped back, reached out, grasped the leg of a small stool at his right. The figure moved toward him. Montague raised the stool to strike. 'Any funny business an' I'll bloody kill you, mate! Now keep back!'

The figure stopped.

Heart pounding, Montague watched transfixed as the dark intruder lifted a hand to remove his hat. The hairless head was little more than a skull encased in parchment flesh. Montague gasped. The stool slipped from his hand to thump upon the carpet. The face was hollow and pallid in the glow cast from the bar. Drawing back into the ludicrous imitation of a grin, the lips revealed a cavernous mouth set with long teeth of skeletal whiteness.

'Who - who are you?' repeated Montague, his voice ebbing to a hoarse whisper.

'Who are you!' grated the mocking voice. 'Who are you, he asks. Why, dear Monty, you know who I am. You know me very well indeed!' Breath rattled. Teeth clicked. The figure moved closer. 'You made me what I am, Monty, old boy. Aren't you proud? Aren't you proud of your creation? You did a fine job, Monty. Oh, yes, a fine job. You lived the life that should have been mine. A good life, too, Monty, whilst I remained a shadow. A life that never was. Now it is time to redress the balance. Monty, dear fellow, I have returned to claim what was rightly mine!'

Montague raised his arms. 'No! It's impossible! You're a bleedin' madman! A freak! Get away from me! Get away!'

Montague would have turned, would have fled back to the imagined sanctuary of the bar, but his foot caught the discarded stool. With a shout he staggered back against a small table, toppled it aside then fell heavily upon his back. The room whirled and when it steadied, the skull-head and empty eyes hovered close above. 'Yes, Monty, old boy,' it cackled, 'to claim what is mine! To claim what is mine!'

His mouth gaped as a vacant smile; the ghastly parody of a Greek comedy mask. Above Montague, the coat fell open to spread as bat wings. Within, there was only blackness - a blackness above which swayed the leering nightmare face. About Montague the bizarre echo rang. 'To claim what is mine! To claim what is mine! To claim what is mine!' It rang until the words struck as a hammer-blow. And wider spread the blackness.

***

'Heart attack?' queried the inspector. 'Bit young for that wasn't he?'

'He wasn't a healthy man,' replied the doctor. 'Flabby and overweight. I've seen 'em go younger, especially in recent years. Dear me, yes.'

They observed the ashen yet wide-eyed features of Montague for the last time as the white sheet was drawn over the body. Outside, a small crowd had gathered by the ambulance. The inspector stepped over to the counter where two of the staff waited, both visibly shaken.

'Well lads?' asked the inspector. 'Have you checked everything?'

'Yes sir,' replied one, 'we don't think nothing's missing.'

'Didn't expect there would be,' muttered the inspector. 'Do either of you know who owns that grey coat we found near the body?'

'The coat? No, but people are always leaving stuff behind - umbrellas and such.'

'All right, lads, you might as well make yourselves scarce. I don't expect the pub will be opening for a while.'

The two departed then, 'Good morning!' interrupted a new voice.

The inspector turned to meet the smile of the young man who had just entered.

'The brewery called half an hour ago and said I was to get down here straight away. Got held up in the traffic, I'm afraid.'

'Ah, yes,' responded the inspector. 'When we rang them they said someone would be available to sort the place out.'

'They didn't say exactly what happened,' continued the newcomer, eyeing the stretcher as it was manoeuvred through the door into bright daylight.

'Heart attack sometime around midnight,' replied the inspector. 'The two lads found him this morning.'

'God, that's awful,' muttered the young man. 'Bad timing, too. I understand he was due for a promotion. Ah, well, I suppose we'll have things up and running again pretty soon.'

'Are you here for the time being then, sir? Neither of the lads said anything.'

'Sorry,' smiled the young man, 'I ought to have introduced myself properly. I'm the assistant manager. I was due to take over the Skinner's Arms when Mr Powell moved on. The name's Rafferty! Patrick Rafferty. The brewery has all my details if you care to check.'

Volcano

'If anyone finds out, Frank, it'll be the end for us both. You know it will.'

She swung around from the window to face him, arms folded tightly, lips slightly parted as though she wished to say more but dared not. In her early thirties, she was slim and beautiful. To him she was a prize worth great risk. In the heavy silence that followed, the spectre of a deed as yet unfulfilled threatened to undermine her resolve. She turned back to the window and gazed across the jumbled little village of ancient stone and terracotta that lay clustered about the hillside under a cobalt haze. So satisfying in its picturesque, haphazard geometry. The sunlit bay beyond reached out to embrace a silver tinsel sea. So innocent.

'How could they find out?' came his voice from behind. 'How? There'd be no clues, no weapons, not a scrap of evidence, nothing. It has to be the perfect - well – you know what I'm saying.'

'The perfect murder, Frank!' she responded, her blue eyes blazing as she spun about to face him once more. 'Why don't we say it? Murder! If we can't even bring ourselves to say the word, we don't stand a chance in hell, do we!'

Dark-haired, clean–shaven Frank, a little older than her, stood with hands thrust awkwardly into his pockets. 'Lay off it, Carol! I'm a bag of bloody nerves, too. You've only got to say forget it - just say it and I will. If I thought you weren't one hundred percent behind me then -.'

Carol stepped across the small bedroom, cupped his face in her hands, looked searchingly into his eyes and kissed him. 'Frank – sweetheart, I'm sorry for being so on edge. If only there was some other way. If only things didn't have to be like this.'

'Yes, Carol, that's the problem, isn't it. There is no other way – not that I can see. I've spent sleepless nights thinking about it – believe me I have. He's got a gun at both our heads: me through my business dealings and you through control over your investments. Why you ever let Gerald put *those* in his own name I'll never know.'

'At the time I trusted him, that's why. If we're all allowed one big mistake in life then that was mine. I admit it. I damn well have to!'

'All right, Carol, I'm sorry. I shouldn't blame you, not when I walked into the same trap with my eyes wide open. Bloody fool I was! At least you have the excuse that you're married to him. I was only looking for an accountant to keep my books looking respectable. Someone with a bit of imagination. Well, Gerald had that all right.'

'You were pushing your luck, Frank, you really were. Even I could see that - though I suppose you could say he was useful in ironing those tax problems of yours out.'

'Yes he was useful. Very useful - as long as I never queried his fees. I can't be the only one to have taken the bait. There must be other people he's got his hooks into, Carol. There have to be!'

'Then look at it this way, Frank – perhaps we're doing them a favour as well as ourselves.'

'Yes,' he breathed, shifting uneasily but remaining close to the spot he had occupied since she had entered his hotel room some minutes earlier, 'I suppose we could look at it like that but it might help matters if some of those other people were sharing the risk.'

'Perhaps, but as you say, you should be completely in the clear once - once it's done.'

'Let's hope the weather's on our side. Let's hope it's like it was when I went up there a few years back. Let's hope I keep my damned nerve.'

'You're a strong lad, Frank, but if it doesn't happen - if you decide at the last moment not to do it, I'll understand. I really will.' She kissed his cheek. 'It won't make any difference to my feelings, love, I promise. We'll find a way sooner or later. We have to, don't we?'

'If I pull this off, Carol, nothing must change for a fair while afterwards. We mustn't even be seen together. That wouldn't look good at all.'

'I'm well aware of that,' She turned again to the window, stared into the distance then glanced at her watch. 'I'd better get going. Gerald will be winding up his game of golf about now and Amanda will be on her way back from the shops.'

'Hmm, Amanda,' he responded thoughtfully. 'My wife's the innocent one in all this.'

'It's a problem you'll have to face eventually, Frank - we both know that.'

'Quite, but eventually isn't right now. By the way, you realise she won't be expecting to go with us tomorrow. Are you both -?'

'I persuaded Amanda to catch the bus with me and spend the morning in Taormina.' she answered, lifting her shoulder bag from the bed, 'We'll have lunch in the old town. There's a show at the Roman theatre so I'll get tickets for that - for all four of us. Then either way, darling, either way -.'

'Yes,' he breathed, as she opened the door to leave, 'either way.'

***

'Quite a view Frank, eh? Quite a view. The girls don't know what they're missing!'

'Amanda never enjoyed going up in one of these things. She gets too scared.'

Pale sunlight filtered through the enclosed space of the cable car to dapple the faces of its only two occupants. Frank had not expected they would be alone together on the way up. Frank had no desire to hold conversation with Gerald at that stage.

'Scared, you say. Poor girl, eh, Frank. Poor girl! Still, I thought Carol would have been game.' His eyes were magnified pale blue behind thick gold-rimmed lenses. He smiled and his mouth, clean-shaven, small but with plumped lips, reminded Frank of a picture once seen in a biology textbook - the life-sucking head of a pallid hagfish. Over the months he had viewed Gerald with growing revulsion and frequently asked himself how an attractive and outward going woman like Carol could have ended up with an obese, bald-headed accountant who, having encouraged the financial misdemeanours of others, then contrived to profit by it. Here was a vampire sucking the financial blood of the unwary.

Gerald's smile twisted into a sly grin. 'Maybe they've got off with a couple of them greasy looking buggers from't bar while we're up 'ere, Frank, eh? What do they call 'em - gigglios is it?

'Gigolos, Gerald.'

'Aye, that's 'em Frank - gigolos! Ruddy dago ponces if you ask me! Let's ring the girls on our mobiles shall we, and see what they're up to and tell 'em what they're missing.'

'Leave it, Gerald,' said Frank, seeing the other reach into his jacket pocket. 'They've gone to the Roman theatre. They won't be too popular if their phones start up in the middle of something.'

Their car bumped gently over the next pylon. A sea of dark volcanic rubble drifted below.

'I 'ope these things are safe Frank, it looks 'ell of a way down to me.'

'I wouldn't worry, Gerald, they carry thousands of people up Mount Etna every month without a problem. We're not very far above the ground at all. Not really.'

'Oh, not really. Not very far? Well I'm sure you're right Frank. Aye, I'm sure you are.'

Gerald twisted his rotund form about, looked to observe another cable car directly behind their own, with a third close behind that.

'Oh, 'eck! Three red'uns in a row!' He turned a grinning-moon face back to his companion. 'Reminds me of ruddy buses back 'ome - three at a time or none at all!'

'I wasn't aware you ever used the buses,' remarked Frank, watching another triplet of red cars sway by on the journey downwards. For a minute, neither spoke, though Gerald peered hard through the windows, his head switching from side to side as though in anticipation of some impending event.

He turned with unnerving suddenness. 'I'm glad we could all make this 'oliday together, Frank.

The two girls are having a grand time and I 'ope it might help iron out a few misunderstandings you and I have experienced. And we've 'ad a few, Frank, make no mistake - I know that. Yes, we've 'ad a few.' His face loomed uncomfortably close. Light glared from his spectacles. 'But, let me say this, I learned my lesson the 'ard way and so must we all. I tell you, there's buggers back 'ome would give a lot to get one over me, Frank, but they never will. Never. I've been too ruddy smart for 'em. Too ruddy smart! Remember, always go in one door an' come out t'other. Keep 'em guessing. Catch 'em by surprise! In one door, Frank - out t'other!'

'You always seem to manage it, Gerald, I'll grant you that.'

'Aye, well, that's business, Frank. That's survival. But I'm not sorry to leave it all behind for a week or so. No, not sorry at all.'

'And you can still keep an eye on me, Gerald – is that it?'

'Eh, that's not a very nice thing to say, Frank. Business is business and 'oliday is 'oliday - and be fair now, it were more your idea than it were mine. You chose this part of the world - it would never 'ave occurred to us. I was never one for exotic places. Miss the 'ome cooking, I do. Plain and 'onest 'ome cooking. None of this dago stuff.'

'I came here with Amanda soon after we first met.' replied Frank. 'I've wanted to come back ever since.'

'Aye, well, it's different I'll grant you that, Frank, especially up 'ere. 'Ello! What's this we're coming to?'

'It's the terminal.'

'Terminal, Frank! Terminal!' he repeated whilst effecting an expression of stark incredulity. 'But we're not at ruddy top yet!'

'No, Gerald, we change here - I mean literally. At the cable station we change shoes for boots and get a warm coat each.'

'Warm coat and boots in this weather - get away!'

'You'll see. We're two thousand five hundred metres up now, and it's another seven hundred odd to the top. There's ice up there most of the year round.'

'Ruddy metres! What's that in English, Frank? And I hope we can get a decent cup of tea before t'next bit.'

'Oh, we'll get something, Gerald, there's a self-service restaurant – or there was.'

Despite their confinement, Frank regretted the need to stop. The journey was longer than he remembered and though trying to affect a degree of normality he feared some unguarded comment or careless gesture might ignite within Gerald a flame of suspicion. The cable car shuddered into its bay and they emerged onto black earth to find themselves amongst a small group of tourists, some speaking English, others not, but all intent on crowding into the restaurant before the last stage of the journey.

'By 'eck it is cooler and no mistake!' puffed Gerald. 'Just like you said it would be, eh, Frank.'

* * *

Revving hard, the minibus creaked and swayed its way up the cinder track leading to the misted ramparts of the volcano's summit.

'Over to the left,' announced their driver and guide in musical Italian accent, 'you can see the old pylons. Now they are part covered in ash. Once, the cable-way goes up to the top, but since the big eruptions of past years, people must walk or go by the bus!'

'It's getting foggy,' observed Gerald as they bumped along.

'We're heading up through the clouds,' replied Frank, inwardly reassured by the encroaching mist. 'It's often like this in the summer. Wintertime it can be clear as a bell. People ski on these slopes.'

'Ski, Frank? On top of a ruddy inferno? Eh, whatever next.'

The bus crunched onto a levelled area already occupied by three other vehicles and numerous visitors, some wearing bright yellow protective helmets.

'Looks ruddy dangerous to me,' remarked Gerald, 'some of those lads are wearing hard hats, Frank. D'you see – hard hats?'

'Don't worry, Gerald, they're going where it's needed - we're not.'

'Please, ladies and gentlemen!' announced the guide, 'We get out and walk around for half an hour but I talk to you first!'

After disembarking they gathered about him, buttoning heavy coats against a chill wind that blustered across the bleak, monochrome landscape. Low clouds scurried in ragged fragments against a paler, slower moving grey. Now and again the higher clouds parted to reveal a glimpse of bright blue sky. Pools of sunlight scampered across, picking out white pockets of ice embedded in gritty basalt.

'Ladies and gentlemen,' resumed the guide, 'we are at an altitude of three thousand, three hundred metres and the air is thin. You should take care not to hurry or make a big exertion. If you have not gone to this height before, it will take away the breath!'

'Them ruddy metres again,' grated Gerald close to Frank's ear. 'What the 'ell's that in yards, feet and ruddy inches?'

Frank shivered at the touch of his breath. The chill he felt was more than the chill of the mountain. 'Er, best part of eleven thousand feet,' he replied.

'Also,' continued their guide, 'you should not go too far away from here! And it is *molto pericoloso* - very dangerous to go close to the edge of any crater!'

'Where are those people going?' asked a young man in their party.

The guide turned. The rest peered beyond him to where the ground, shrouded intermittently in vapour, ascended more steeply to a curving black ridge. A group of six people in drab anoraks were observed making their way up toward the ridge, bright yellow helmets bobbing against the darkly looming bulk. As those below watched, there came a boom of distant thunder, emanating not from the sky but from the mountain's innards. A cascade of fragments arched up, a dark flock against shifting clouds, most falling back into the gaping maw that had spawned them, some plummeting to the flanks of the cone where they tumbled, smoking, to the lower slopes. The six diminutive figures climbed on undaunted.

The guide returned to his small audience. 'Where those people go is the north-east crater. This crater is very dangerous. Always there is something happening. Those people, they go on their own without a guide. Even wearing the hard hat is no good if a big piece of lava comes down on the head!'

Most of the party laughed as he waggled a clenched fist over his own head and grinned widely. 'So is no good to go up there for us!'

'There's nowt'd get me up there with that stuff flyin' around, hat or no,' rumbled Gerald. 'Daft buggers, eh, Frank. Daft buggers.'

As if to bolster his sentiment, there occurred another abyssal detonation, this time followed by a ragged plume of black smoke, from the flanks of which descended another shower of fragments.

'So now I tell you,' their guide went on, 'Etna - she is not one Volcano but many on one mountain. The big craters are on top and the smaller ones you saw below when first you arrived near the cable car. Some craters do nothing - they are asleep for a time and others, they always erupt. That way,' he pointed to his left, 'is the central crater. Always smoke is coming out of it. That you should visit. Now we walk about and we can look. Remember please! Do not go far away and do not go close to the edge of the craters!'

The small party fanned out. Only two remained behind with the guide.

'Well, are you going to show me about while we're up 'ere, Frank?' asked Gerald. 'We 'aven't a lot of time and you should know the way.'

'Yes, Gerald, let's take a look over the central crater first.'

The clouds were driving down to obscure a sombre landscape in shrouds of vapour as they set off. Cold drizzle spattered their faces.

'Oh, 'eck, this is worse than ruddy Pennines in November,' grated Gerald from behind as they trudged upward. 'Sight of a lifetime is it, Frank? That's what you said on't way up. Sight of a lifetime. I bloody 'ope so after all this palaver.'

'It'll most likely clear again soon.' answered Frank.

They crunched along the cinder path in obscuring mist. The bus that had brought them was by then out of sight. The world closed in and they found themselves quite alone. All was going to plan yet Frank feared his thoughts were bold enough to materialise as a ghost in the mist and whisper on the breeze his dire intentions. Words rang in his mind as if spoken loudly. 'You've put years on me, Gerald. Made my life a bloody misery. You've enjoyed twisting my guts and you've never given a damn about Carol. Yes, Carol – she's no more than a bloody status symbol. You're a shit, Gerald. A bloody parasite. Nobody ever managed to catch you out. You always wriggled back into the woodwork and some other poor bastard caught it. Not this time, Gerald! No, by God - not this time!'

'Are you all right, Frank?' broke in the voice from behind.

'What?'

'You were talking to yourself. Is something up?'

'Talking to -? No, I didn't say anything. Just humming a tune or so.'

The two stopped. Wind blustered all about but the drizzle was easing.

'Is something up, Frank?' Gerald repeated, standing much too close, glasses reflecting in miniature a parade of oily rag clouds. 'Why lad, you're white as a ruddy sheet!'

Frank took a deep breath then continued on. 'It's the altitude, Gerald,' he remarked, over his shoulder. 'We'll be there in a minute. We'll be at the crater.'

'Well, well - and I imagined I'd be the one to suffer from't ruddy altitude, not our experienced traveller! Eh, that is a surprise, Frank. That is a surprise!'

Another boom and the mists began to lighten, retreating as the drizzle eased for a time. The crater rim ahead was becoming visible, the world beginning to open out as the clouds dispersed. As if to illuminate a surreal stage, sunlight flooded through. It was just as Frank remembered. A vast breathing organ from whose grim depths issued a column of spectral vapour. Through this could be seen the far edge of the crater. On the edge of that terrible void his options were stark as the landscape. If Frank did nothing they would retrace their steps downward and the nightmare would continue. Carol had said she would understand but that could solve nothing. Failure would haunt him and in the end Gerald might destroy them both.

Frank folded his arms and stood as close to the gently curving edge as he dared. 'What d'you think of this, Gerald? Impressed?'

'Oh aye, Frank, very interesting. Not much good as real estate though. Just a big 'ole in the ground.' His face broke into a grin. 'Not close enough t'ruddy shops either.'

Gerald, too, stepped a little nearer the edge.

Frank looked about. There were people visible through the smoke haze at the far side of the crater but no one in evidence nearby. He noted a small party trudging downward on the curve of another path but they would soon be out of sight. Close to his foot lay an amorphous lump of black rock. The clouds were returning and in moments they would be totally obscured from view. Frank stooped to grasp the rock with a trembling hand.

'What the 'ell are you up to now, Frank?' Gerald peered down quizzically at him.

'Up to? Oh, I'm taking back a souvenir of our visit,' replied Frank hoarsely. 'I'll get it polished and made into a paperweight.'

'Oh, aye, Frank - a paperweight is it? Then pick one out for me as well. Handy things, paperweights.'

Another boom rolled through thickening mist as Frank arose. The booming filled his head. An echoing rage. Gerald continued to watch him. Frank's grip loosened on the rock. He was about to let it fall when someone on the now obscured far side of the crater called out and Gerald turned to look.

Frank caught his breath and gripped the basalt clump hard. The world had become unreal as he spun about to swing the rock against the side of Gerald's head. A crack of splitting bone and Gerald staggered about, his glasses swinging preposterously from one ear whilst from the gaping mouth emerged a child's cry. For a moment he continued swaying, across his face a spreading arabesque of bright blood. He reached out a hand but Frank dropped the stone then hurled himself against Gerald, thrusting him toward the crater rim. With a feline howl, Gerald collapsed in a shower of black grit, feet kicking, fingers clawing frantically at cinders that crumbled in his grasp, sliding further over the edge, his gaze upon Frank. Astonished. Disbelieving.

Then, he was gone.

Frank remained transfixed, waiting for a cry or a scream from within that terrible abyss.

There was only silence.

He moved to the edge but it was impossible to peer far into the crater through ever-rising vapours. Already the ash was giving way under his feet. Frank backed away and gazed into silent mists. No one could have seen them from the other side of the crater. No one could have witnessed what had happened. With the toe of his shoe, he rolled the blood-wetted basalt lump to the edge. It, too, vanished from sight.

Minutes passed before Frank set off downward from the crater to retrace his steps - their steps. He was cold, the clouds were thickening and light rain spattered his face. Rain! He glanced up at the clouds. Could it rain hard enough to quell the fires he imagined must burn down there? Yes - quell the fires and reveal the stricken body? 'Don't be bloody stupid,' he breathed, hurrying on. 'That's impossible. Impossible!'

There were three people waiting at the minibus. He might appear to them pale and uneasy but the cold and altitude would account for that. He could make out the figure of their guide approaching through the mist and in conversation with another couple from their party. 'Too bad it is raining now.' said the guide as Frank joined them. 'We wait for the others and then we go down.'

'Did Gerald - did the man I was with find you?' Frank asked.

'No, *signore*, I have not seen him. He will be with the other two I think.'

A young man and woman appeared out of the mists, laughing, talking loudly in German.

'Your friend, he is not with them,' remarked the guide, 'but he must come soon.'

'I think he was looking for you,' said Frank. 'He wanted to get back to the bus. He could be lost.'

The guide glanced at his watch. 'We cannot leave until he is here, *signore*. Does he have a mobile phone?'

'I'm sure he does,' replied Frank, 'but I don't know his number.'

'Then we must try to find him.'

'All right,' said Frank, turning about, 'I'll head back the way I came.'

'Wait!' called the guide. 'What is this man's name?'

'It's Gerald. Gerald Carruthers.'

'Car-roo-therz,' repeated the guide. 'Signor Car-roo-therz!'

'That's it,' responded Frank, 'Carruthers.'

'OK - please,' continued the guide, 'other people can help but someone must stay here in case he returns. That one will have my card and my mobile number.'

The guide stayed with Frank and for twenty minutes they searched, working in pairs, calling into grey, drenching mist whilst the volcano answered with intermittent thunder.

'Your friend,' queried the guide, 'he often goes alone?'

'Alone? I really can't say. I've never been away with him before.'

When they re-emerged from the mists on the sloping apron between the north-east and central craters, the guide peered at his watch, '*Signore*, we must return to the bus. I must report this. Others will have to come and look for your friend. This is very bad!'

'I'm sorry, I don't know why Gerald should -.' He was cut short by a hollow detonation. The ground shook and the two began to hurry. Something hissed through the air with banshee howl. Too late, the guide saw it descend spinning out of the mist to strike Frank squarely in the back, hurling him with a high-pitched shriek and a cascade of black grit down the slope toward the parking area. There, he rolled over and lay still.

No one could doubt Frank was dead as they gathered about. Rain-sodden and begrimed, his rag-doll body lay sprawled face up, limbs absurdly twisted, dirt-filled eyes gazing sightless into rolling clouds. Blood oozed from gaping jaws that remained frozen in mid-scream. And whilst the guide called urgently over his phone, the onlookers remained silent in a chill rain.

***

Two hours passed before his body was carried into the mortuary. Now it rested face down on the cold slab. A hand reached out, lifted the white sheet, pulled it down to reveal the rear of the head and bruised, pallid shoulder.

'Never have I witnessed anything like this,' said the doctor with a puzzled nod of his head. 'It is a quite remarkable occurrence, I am sure you will agree.'

'I understand he was struck by a fragment from the volcano,' said the police inspector. 'I assume that was the cause of his death.'

'Yes, a molten fragment ejected from the crater. It was a million to one chance from so great a distance, of course. But - but look at this.'

He eased the sheet further from the lifeless form. 'Look where the fragment burned into his flesh. See, it is directly over the heart.'

'My God!' breathed the inspector, peering close. 'It is the perfect shape of a human hand.'

Secret

In a harsh and desolate part of the world existed a chasm, a narrow crack in the surface of the land but one that went very deep. Deeper than anyone ever knew. The chasm was not wide – measuring at its greatest no more than an arm's length. In times of winter freezing and spring thawing, a piece of earth or rock might crumble away and plummet into depths of eternal blackness. In times of strong, dry wind when the air was warmer, a curtain of dust might descend in silence to the abyss. And although during a part of the year sunlight would spear into the chasm, never could it strike far enough to illuminate beyond the uppermost reaches.

A short way below the rim an irregular, meandering ledge followed the gap of this crevasse for a modest distance. Where the ledge was at its widest, somewhat wider than a human hand, a flower grew amidst a small cluster of green leaves in soil that had accumulated there; a flower whose petals of luminous crimson grew paler toward edges patterned by pure white striations. It peered upward to a welcome sun whose traverse across the sky followed the line of the fissure during the mildest part of the year. Its shallow roots were nourished by moisture trapped and percolating slowly through the rock wall from melted winter snow and rare showers of rain.

When bitter winters fell across the earth above to render it stark white and bereft of movement, a gentle current rising from deep within subterranean realms nurtured the roots with a breath of warmth. The flower would fade and be reborn through the

118

seasons and the years, and when spring burst over the land, when insects took to the air, some would visit the secret abode as darting motes, their wings glittering against sun and sky.

Occasionally, in the distant days of the caravans, people encountered the fissure as they traversed this largely-arid land, and when they did it was nearly always during the short summer months. Except for small children, those who cared or dared to, would stride across or jump the gap even at its widest. On passing by, most regarded this fissure in the ground with little more than brief curiosity. Now and again someone might pause to cast a stone, a coin or a token into impenetrable blackness then stooping over the edge, listen to the diminishing rattle of its downward progress. Others, on contemplating the fearsome depths, were afraid for themselves, for their young and for their animals and so preferred to skirt about until finding the chasm no more than a narrow gap in the ground, if not vanished altogether.

When caravans with oxen, horses and wagons crossed above the chasm their voices rose and fell as the drivers urged their beasts on. The rumble of their wheels shivered the ground, spilling grit into the void as the wagons crossed. The children they would lift up and carry in case one should disappear forever into black nightmare depths they had no wish to contemplate.

On a rare day of oppressive heat, in a half forgotten age, a bright-eyed child peered over the side. He noticed the petals shining in sunlight and, having bravely jumped the gap, reached down to grasp the flower, all but blotting out the sky above the ledge where it grew. The flower lay just beyond his outstretched hand. He tried to reach further down, straining to touch with outspread fingers when a woman cried out. Hands seized and he was dragged away protesting whilst others strode across, casting shadows over the ledge with no concern for the object of the boy's desires.

Caravans, sometimes a lone traveller continued to pass that way but never through the endlessly turning wheel of seasons did another pay attention to that bright splash of colour poised above the chasm depths.

One spring the caravans and travellers failed to appear. In their place horsemen rode across the plain, most of them some distance from the crevasse though the thunder of their hooves reverberated deep within it. The land lay quiet through a brief summer. A morning in early autumn of that same year was greeted by braying horns, drums and the tramp of marching feet – by far a greater number than had ever before passed by.

Soon after, the day was rent by conflict and commotion. And although not so close, the clash of arms drifted through the air above the chasm. Men cried out, some in triumph, others in agony through a din of confusion that spread as a tide over the world above. Men hurried by in both directions – some advancing, others retreating in panic. The clamour lasted into the night then diminished until the pitiful cries of the stricken were all that remained to greet a rising sun.

Later that morning more horsemen arrived and stayed for a time, the sounds of their presence remaining until the sun was close to the western horizon. With their departure, silence returned. But in the warm days that followed the air was tainted by vapours of death. Keen-eyed vultures and other carrion birds circled the skies and descended. The sound of their raucous squabbles with other scavengers of raw flesh drifted across the chasm.

Shortly after daybreak in a later year when breezes of spring played above and birds of a different kind, broad-winged and long necked, crossed the sky in formation, when the flower was beginning to bloom, many people, animals and carts proceeded across the plain in disordered haste. Their wagons were burdened with whatever food and belongings they had managed to gather for their fear induced journey. Horses and oxen snorted, hooves and wagon wheels, crossing the fissure where it was of little hazard, sent stones to clatter echoing, fading ever deeper into blackness.

They continued by throughout much of that morning when one of the horse-drawn wagons, heavily burdened but driven by urgency rather than by caution, pushed from behind by ragged men and youths, attempted to lumber over the crevasse where it was widest. As it passed above, a rear wheel struck hard against the edge then split apart. The wagon stopped, heeling over to obscure shafts of sunlight that had until that moment fallen across the ledge. Men and women yelled aloud as they scurried back and forth. Children wailed as people strode in haste across the chasm to the rear of the wagon. The shouting continued whilst many strained in desperation, some to push, others to drag the wagon clear of the edge, dislodging fragments and grit to cascade close by the flower.

When eventually the wagon lurched forward a number of small items, followed by copper pans and pottery dishes, spilled from it, clanging, rattling loudly as they vanished into oblivion. The wagon no longer blotted out light but anxious voices filled the air from close above together with the sound of urgent hammering. They were still there when the sun was past its zenith and where the flower shimmered had fallen into shadow.

Only when darkness brimmed fully over the narrow ledge were they gone.

Part way through the next morning, when sunlight returned to probe the fissure, many horsemen swept across the land. Those taking the wider gap did so with ease, the thud of galloping hooves, the ring of their weapons echoing within its depths.

Years rolled by before others returned to disturb the solitude. These were people of a different tongue, people who travelled in smaller groups from spring through much of autumn with their beasts of burden. They passed through countless seasons, never stopping, usually skirting the chasm where the flower thrived in regal colour. Eventually these later caravans also ceased and the chasm sighed to passing breezes, through quiet ages.

One day, from a distance came sounds; not of people but of machines. A distant droning not unlike that of the summer insects.

Soon after, on a calm summer day, a speck appeared high in the air above the chasm, approaching, receding, crossing and re-crossing, buzzing louder than a bee as it wheeled against the sky. From that day on, over the passing years, there were more, many flying higher, some buzzing louder. In time they were more distant still - just silver glints passing high with a distant rumble, intersecting the river of sky above the crevasse with trails of white vapour that slowly drifted, spread and dispersed.

The years flickered by and except in deepest of winters a distant, occasional rumble that had long ago replaced the thud of hooves, carried on. The trails in the sky increased regardless of season when the flower, its petals gone, lay dormant and nurtured by the womb of Earth.

Another spring arrived but the world had changed. When the flower awoke, expanded and opened to greet sunlight and warmer air, the rumble had ceased. White, diaphanous skeins no longer threaded a peaceful sky. Vortices of anger shivered the air and swept across the land. The ground about the chasm trembled to a growl of engines. Dark shadows sped fleetingly across the sky above, each followed by a crash of thunder that was answered by a bellow from deep within the chasm.

The earth shook with the approach of machines, the like of which the land had never known. Most passed at a distance from the fissure but one crossed above it in shattering fury close to where the flower stood, its metal tracks grinding earth, dislodging rock fragments and grit from the chasm edge to plunge clattering down amidst clouds of swirling dust.

In the wake of those machines followed others more distant. More shadows blinked across the sky with booming in their wake until the sun was low.

After darkness there were more. Lightning flashed above and thunder rolled where there were no storm clouds at all.

One morning the sounds were gone. The following days ushered a return to calm. But soon after came darker skies and a reddened sun that no longer kept its promise of warmth for the coming summer. The days that followed became darker and colder so that the flower faded and shrunk away. Ghosts of winter haunted the land above yet still the chasm exhaled the tempered warmth of deepest earth. The ghosts above became real and remained to shroud the land in white. The years turned but the winter of heavy skies would not retreat.

When the cold and dark at last began to wane, when the sun was higher and pale tendrils of light reached into the chasm, a trickle of water began some way along from the ledge. The mantle of a long winter was wearing thin, exorcized by returning warmth. Over coming days, with the sky no longer obscured, long banished spring emerged.

On the ledge life stirred. A green shoot struggled toward the sky. It strengthened, budded then began to open. The flower bloomed once more. In its innocence and in its purity it returned, secret of a lifeless land. It blossomed as a beacon with vivid, smiling petals to greet a new day, a new season where only peace reigned. Yet ghosts of what had passed were still in the winds. Ghosts that sparked the plant with new pulses of life.

The days wore on and further along the ledge, where nothing had grown before, new shoots struggled toward the light, their growth kindled by a radiation born by the breezes, and soft rains that for the first time brought moisture to an ageless aridity. Other shoots appeared, now at ground level on both sides of the crevasse. In time, as the world grew warmer and the harsher winters declined, they spread all along the chasm edge and across its walls in blazing curtains of white-edged crimson. As the seasons rolled by, as the insects returned, more flowers colonised the land, spreading outward amidst fields of grass, their seeds taking to the skies.

In time the flower would spread unhindered to grace the warm and fertile regions of the planet, mutating in form, colour and size, brushing field, hillside and ruined city with vibrant colour. But wherever in the world they thrived, there would be no one to see.

Lighthouse

'We ought not to be taking this course,' said the second officer looking out at the grey, restless sea through which the SS *Black Swan* was heading. 'For the sake of half a day it's too great a risk.'

'I have made our situation perfectly clear have I not?' replied the captain. 'This is the most important, the most lucrative voyage this vessel has so far undertaken. We have on board over fifty extremely wealthy people together with their staff. They intend - no, they are determined to celebrate our queen's diamond jubilee in the manner to which they are suited. We are running behind schedule and the company most certainly risks penalties should we have them ashore later than the time agreed.'

'A piece of flotsam damaging our rudder can hardly be blamed on us or on the company,' responded his second officer. 'And might I add that the repair was only temporary. Yes, rather too temporary for my liking from what I saw of it.' The concern in his voice was plainly evident.

'As you say, Mr Campbell, damage to the rudder was no fault of ours but I doubt such an excuse would impress those parting with their cash – unearned or no! We count a distant cousin of Queen Victoria herself amongst our passengers. Cancelling this voyage would have brought financial ruin upon the company.'

'The weather may be moderate to the likes of us,' said the second officer, 'but there were two or three of 'em up on deck heaving their innards over the side last time I looked out.'

'I'm inclined to blame that on over indulgence, Mr Campbell. Even should it be otherwise, the weather is hardly something they can blame us for. And this is not the first vessel I've taken through these straits – no it is not. D'you remember the *Flamingo*?'

'I do remember her, captain, but that voyage was in August when the straits are calmer. We are now in late October when the situation is far less certain - and it will be dark long before we pass the Bale Rocks to our starboard. Charts or no, these waters are treacherous. Conditions are unpredictable.'

'None of this I dispute, Mr Campbell, but the glass has remained steady all day.'

'Well, captain, it's falling now and it is falling quickly.'

'Have confidence, sir – confidence! I see no signs of deterioration in the weather. I believe conditions will remain satisfactory for some time yet and you will recall, the current is in our favour when steaming south.' There was a note of irritation in his voice as he continued, 'Under the circumstances I see *every* reason to avoid our going seaward of the Bale Rocks. By maintaining good speed we will make far better time by taking the landward passage. I'm sure you will enter all of this in your log, Mr Campbell. I, meanwhile, have to go below and make sure all is running smoothly as possible for our worthy guests. I hear the band is fully occupied down there and by midnight the tide of champagne will doubtless have taken their minds off our moderately choppy seas.'

'Keep our course, helmsman,' ordered the second officer, turning to the wheel.

'Very good, sir,' came the reply. 'East of the Bale Rocks it is.' The helmsman gazed resolutely ahead. Already the gaunt cliffs of the promontory arose vaguely to their port. The darkening sky above was smeared by ragged clouds, breaking then reforming in chaotic sweep. The wind was brisk but the sea not yet heavy. The Bale Rocks light he did not expect to observe until some time after eleven o'clock that evening.

***

The Bale Rocks lighthouse had been in sight for some twenty minutes. The captain was still absent from the bridge and midnight was approaching when the helmsman turned in trepidation to the second officer. 'Sir, she's no longer answering to the wheel!'

'What!' exclaimed the second officer. 'What are you saying, man?'

'I'm saying, sir, she's *not* answering to the wheel! We have lost steerage!'

Campbell watched him swing the wheel then exclaimed, 'My God – that blasted rudder!'

Despite the motion of the ship, couples in their finery danced beneath the warm light of swaying chandeliers, stewards hurried back and forth with teetering trays held high. Glass in hand the captain sat in lively conversation at his table amidst the noise and swirl of the celebrations. With the band playing loudly he at first did not hear the officer's summons.

Ten minutes later saw the captain and his second officer joined on the bridge by first officer

Hartley and chief engineer Cobham. The helmsman, grim-faced, remained with his hands dutifully on the now useless wheel.

'The welding repairs we had undertaken in port must have failed,' said Cobham. 'Captain, there's nothing we can do until daylight with the vessel anchored in calmer water. Two men will need to go over the side and assess the problem.'

'And we'll find no other vessel in these waters to hail for assistance,' added Hartley.

The sound of the band could be heard well above the rumble of the engines. The captain stared at his chief engineer for interminable seconds then looked around at the others. 'Then it seems, gentlemen, we have no choice but to put out trust in the current. D'you not agree, Mr Campbell?'

Second officer Campbell did not reply but stood by the helmsman, gazing out into the night. The bale Rocks light was more clearly visible from their swaying vessel. First officer Hartley turned to see what Campbell saw.

'This is madness!' exclaimed Campbell. 'We should drop anchor now!'

'The tide has too much a hold on us to drop anchor,' declared Hartley. 'Heading this close to the Bale Rocks means we may have to abandon ship! We have to warn everyone below!

'We can't lower the boats – not here!' responded Campbell. 'The sea in these straits is too treacherous and the wind is increasing!'

'But we *have* to tell them!' insisted Hartley.

'And what d'you expect them to do,' retorted the captain, angrily, 'pack their belongings and line up waiting for the gangway?'

'But we can't just -!' blurted the first officer.

'No – I say, no!' countered the captain. 'We keep our engines running full ahead. The tide will help carry us through. It's flowing quicker now the straits are close to their narrowest. After that we'll weigh anchor in calmer waters.'

'The tide, Captain!' exclaimed Campbell. 'D'you realise what you have done? Whether we go full ahead, full astern or stop the engines it will make no difference at all. There's a good chance this tide will carry us onto the Bale Rocks!'

'Damn you, man!' bellowed the captain. 'If any of you've a better idea then let me hear it! Otherwise we maintain our speed – there's nothing else for it until we are clear of the straits. Nothing! Let their damned party go on!'

'Yes, let it go on,' muttered Campbell. 'Let it go on into eternity with the rest of us.'

***

The tower, a major engineering feat of the early 1860's, arose stark white into the sky from the sometimes visible, often not, gaping black-toothed jaws that were the Bale Rocks. Close to the lighthouse where coal, oil and the boat were kept there nestled a small outhouse. Nothing more could have been built there other than the wooden jetty supported by rough concrete posts. Only via this jetty could a shallow draught boat from the relief ship deliver supplies – weather permitting.

Nathan, having served for many years in Queen Victoria's navy, was now head keeper of the Bale Rocks light. A single man, Nathan could never leave the sea behind, nor did he mind the isolation of this remote place, or the storms with which it was so often and so suddenly beset. To the amusement of his colleagues he utilised much of his off-duty time in making dollhouses and the tiny items of furniture with which to populate them. He would take them ashore when his turn of leave came and offer them to any poor child he considered might derive pleasure from his generosity. As usual that day he had busied himself in the watch room checking the oil level and wicks of the great lantern in readiness for the evening.

Ex-marine stoker, Barney, the second keeper, a little younger than Nathan, had performed his duty of cleaning out and replenishing the cooking range down below with fresh coal from their stores before preparing their afternoon meal. Matt, youngest of the three by only a month or so, and once a trawler deckhand, had spent a part of his day fishing when the tide was low and the sea calmer to supplement their diet. Later in the day he had been precariously occupied outside on the lantern gallery cleaning the storm panes. The weather in the strait at that time had been relatively benign with the tide flowing smoothly. He now slept in the keepers' quarters prior to taking up his eight hourly watch.

At sunset Nathan had lit the lamps behind their Fresnel lenses. Barney had ensured the lead weight that drove the clockwork gears rotating the lantern was wound up to its limit - a strenuous task needing to be undertaken every hour and a half. After dark the lantern would revolve upon its reservoir of mercury, flashing a warning across hostile sea and into desolate night, white-red, white-red, white-red.

The brass-cased clock showed eleven-thirty when Nathan, seated reading in the watch room, heard Barney in conversation with Matt. The latter had just finished what for him counted as breakfast before starting his turn of duty. As he emerged at the top of the wooden spiral stairs, Nathan said, 'Wind's getting up. I reckon we're in for quite a storm and soon.' It was then that Nathan, glancing into the obscurity of night, saw the ship. 'Well I'll be -!' He exclaimed, reaching for his binoculars. 'There's a vessel out there. She's heading through the strait if I'm not mistaken.'

'Looks that way,' agreed Matt, 'she's too close in to turn seaward now.'

'Not a wise course this time of the year,' said Nathan. 'From what I can make out, she's a small passenger ship – one of those so-called pocket liners.'

'I've heard all about pocket liners,' quipped Matt. 'They line the pockets of the owners by hiring 'em to the well-off.'

Nathan called Barney up to join them and as anxious minutes passed they watched the lights of the vessel grow brighter in a sea that was becoming ever more turbulent. The ship drew closer and Nathan said, 'There's something wrong with that vessel, boys. She needs to change her course to port, and pretty soon. They can't have mistaken our light. What's the matter with them?'

'I dunno,' responded Barney, 'but she must turn soon or there's trouble.'

But the ship came on.

The three men pushed through the door onto the gallery into a chill, wildly blustering night. 'Look at her will you!' exclaimed Barney. 'Just look!'

'She's all lit up and making smoke!' cried Matt. 'And music – she's so close you can hear it above the wind and the sea! They're coming on! Why don't they change course?'

'It's too bloody late for that!' responded Nathan. 'At this rate she'll strike within minutes!'

And still the ship came on.

As men frozen they watched the spectacle of horror unfold before them. A crash and screech of metal seared the midnight air. The vessel shuddered and rolled. She lifted with the sea then fell back, booming like thunder amidst a tumult of sea foam. Some of her lights wavered then vanished, others flared bright as fires ignited. She rolled violently, lifted again - then a rending crack of metal.

'Her masts are down!' cried Nathan. 'God Almighty, her back's broken! She's breakin' apart!'

There were shouts and cries. People were emerging into a night awash with cold spray and sea. Some held onto railings, others were swept from tilted decks into dark, growling chaos.

'We have to help them,' yelled Barney, turning to the door. 'We'll get the oilskins! We'll get to them somehow!'

Matt turned to follow him but Nathan called, 'No, lads – don't go down there! There's no way you can reach anyone! The tide's running over the rocks! There's nothing you can do! Nothing!' But they were gone from sight and scrambling down in near darkness to the storeroom.

In sheer despair Nathan might have followed but a thunderous boom reached his ears and he turned to see the vessel split asunder, her stern half rolling aside, her bows capsizing altogether. Her lights were almost gone but cries in the night still continued when from beneath the tower two figures emerged into the chaos of night. They stepped to the edge of the platform, itself awash, then onto the rocks, shouting incoherent words into a raging turmoil.

'Come back you fools!' cried Nathan. 'Come back – you'll not reach anyone out there!'

They did not hear him but clambered on, almost invisible in near blackness. Fearful dark waves arose to surge then brake spectral white over the Bale Rocks, swamping, engulfing anyone still alive until their cries were no longer heard. Nathan leaned over the rail calling repeatedly, 'Barney! Matt!' his voice overwhelmed by the insane tumult of wind and sea. Minutes passed before he pulled back from the rail. He entered the watch room, slammed the door against the nightmare beyond then threw himself into the chair with hands raised to clutch his face. A banshee howl clamoured against the storm panes. Close above him the lantern continued to turn with indifferent clockwork precision, its light spearing into soulless oblivion.

After a time he got up, glanced at the window but saw only his own beleaguered reflection. Outside, the tide was still rising and he knew by morning the wreckage and all those within it or fallen amidst sea and rocks would have been driven clear and swept alive or dead into open water. A sharp ping from the brass bell caused him to turn. The lead weight had to be wound back up. Nathan collected the heavy iron handle from its storage space, slotted it into the gear mechanism and with his back bent, turned it steadily around.

The light must keep turning at all times. At all times – no matter what.

***

The horizon was brightening when the lantern came to rest and Nathan extinguished the wicks. Outside on the gallery the storm had abated to a chilling bluster and the clouds were beginning to dissipate. The deadly teeth of the Bale Rocks were exposed to his gaze once more, hideous black against a white foaming sea. Of the vessel, of the people she had carried and of his two colleagues, there was no sign. In the watch room he waited by the top of the spiral stairs. Had the horror of that previous night been real? Would he soon hear their voices? Would the grinning faces of Barney and Matt appear from below?

Nathan waited. There was the sound of wind and sea. There was the steady ticking of the clock. Nothing more. There were tasks to be attended, but not yet. He retired below to his bunk and lay there thinking over what had happened. No one from the outside world would know what he had witnessed until the relief ship arrived with fresh supplies, newspapers and mail in two weeks' time. Nathan closed his eyes and slept a restless sleep.

Poised on the edge of consciousness he imagined he heard music playing. Imagined there were people talking and laughing somewhere in the distance. He turned over but the sounds carried on until suddenly he was wide awake. Then utter silence. Nathan slid from his bunk and stood breathing the still air. The wall clock told him it was half way through the morning.

135

'There's my duties to get on with,' he murmured. 'The light will be showing tonight as it must. For two weeks I'll be managing here alone but I'll see my light shows tonight and every night. By God, what awful things I've witnessed.'

Nathan slept again that afternoon because he knew he must. And again the dreaming. Again the music and the chatter of people haunted his mind, still vague and distant. He woke up confused but determined to carry on. Each afternoon the oil was replenished and the lantern made ready. Each evening it was lit and through each night, at the signal from the bell, the weight was laboriously wound to keep the lantern turning until the eastern sky brightened.

Through the passing days Nathan ate, worked and slept. And when he slept there were the sounds, each time a little closer, each time a little louder, until he imagined that whilst he slept another world had come into being not far away. Outside his hours of sleep he was unable to dispel the vision of horrors that continued to pass before his eyes. Eventually he was reluctant to step out onto the gallery and look down at the rocks and sea because he feared he might relive with greater intensity the tragedy that so haunted him. When the lantern turned and shone after dark he sat facing it because he could no longer glance over his shoulder into the night.

In sleeping he escaped what the hours of darkness had brought. Instead there were the people, happy people and their music. Louder. Closer. The day came when it persisted after he woke as a faraway echo that remained until he ascended the spiral stairway to the watch room. Another day or so and he could hear it rising from below for much of the time - then all of the day until the music and chatter became almost as real as the sound of wind and the sea. He walked about the galley, gaze fixed to the floor, murmuring, 'What I saw was never so. No, it can't have been so.'

That final morning, with the lantern extinguished, Nathan retired to his bed but could not sleep. From the depths of the tower arose those haunting sounds, seeming by then more real than the world outside; a hostile world of sea and storm he no longer cared to confront. Rising from the bunk he trod slowly down to the storeroom. Only steps away chatter, laughter and music spilled out. Nathan stepped forward. He reached out to open the door.

***

At the court of enquiry the captain of the relief ship was asked his opinion concerning the fate of the *Black Swan* and of the keepers at the Bale Rocks light.

'Swept away - all of 'em I reckon,' he replied. 'Bodies and wreckage have been reported by passing ships in open sea beyond the strait. We may never know what happened out there. Even re-supplying the Bale Rocks light is a risky business. We have to lower our cutter and row up to their jetty even at high tide. That can take more than one trip. We've sometimes had to turn back because of the tides and the weather so they kept extra supplies there just in case.'

He was next asked, 'Then how do you account for the fact that the light was reported showing by the captain of a vessel passing to seaward of the Bale Rocks only hours before your ship arrived? And in your own report you state that the ashes in the cooking range at the lighthouse were still warm.'

'I cannot account for any of that, sir. All I can say is that there was no sign of anyone at the lighthouse when we landed. We searched from top to bottom, from the lantern house to the store room. There was no one at all. No one, I say. And only one set of oilskins was what we found. I left an experienced man with two assistants to maintain the light – men of my own I could ill afford to do without. Fortunately the light was in good order.'

***

But the light was not to continue. Soon after the disaster, and because it was too difficult to maintain and keep supplied, the Bale Rocks lighthouse was abandoned and a new more powerful lighthouse built on the mainland at each end of the strait.

In the lonely and deserted tower, when storms raged at night, the band would play. The dancers would whirl and turn as the lantern once had turned. When the wind screamed in anger, when the waves growled and thundered over the Bale Rocks, the party would begin again.

Apparition

The air hung damp and heavy with an odour of mouldering leaves. Bare trees rose up at the rear and sides of the muted brick house, forlorn in frozen stillness. Forlorn, too, the crows weaving mournful call beneath a leaden sky. Part obscured by a chill mist of early morning, woods and fields spread as a faded, monochrome backdrop. Across this bleak landscape drifted the peel of a distant church bell, calling in measured slowness as a voice burdened by the sorrows of winter.

Before the house waited a coach and pair. Burdened precariously with trunks and boxes, the coach grated and swayed. The horses champed, snorting white vapour, the stamp of their impatient hooves muffled by dead earth. Perched high, the coachman peered ruddy-faced from beneath a wide-brimmed hat, his hunched form laden with overcoat, blanket and muffler.

From the main door of the house emerged two figures, wrapped in heavy capes, one top-hatted, the other wearing a black satin bonnet. The first carried a large canvas and leather bag, the second, a red and gold hatbox, counterpoint to this sombre world in colourful and homely aspect. A young woman dressed in heavy woollen shawl and head-scarf followed several paces behind, carrying two small suitcases which she rested for a moment on the doorstep so as to grasp the cold iron door knocker. The door boomed shut with a final, hollow echo.

Their cases stowed at the rear, the three clambered into the coach and slammed the door. A grunt of vapoured air arose from the coachman. At the coach window a face appeared, bright-eyed, her hand wiping misted glass, her bonnet removed so that she might press close and gaze upon the house this one last time. The whip raised, hissed and cracked over the horses. A sharp call from the coachman and the coach strained, creaked then began to rumble forward. Rocking gently, it moved along the curve of the path, soon to disappear beyond the trees.

Empty. Silent. The house stood alone with its terrible secret.

***

Life returned in time and the house knew seasons, years and changing generations. Gone were smoking candles, the reek of paraffin, the spitting of coal fires and tapping of shoes upon a bare stone kitchen floor. Other sounds, other lights, other lives flourished within the walls. But still no one knew. Leaves were falling from ancient trees that still guarded the house. Trees taller and fewer than the trees that once stood there. The same church bell chimed its call through autumn air, now in remorse for the passing of a half forgotten age.

***

A naked light bulb glared from the centre of the room. It did nothing to alleviate the harshness of exposed floorboards nor the unwelcoming monotony of bare walls, in spite of ornate cornice mouldings and newly stripped skirting boards. Two leather easy chairs occupied the centre of the room, together with a mahogany and glass coffee table, and before them, the blank facade of a silent television. Close by, a small electric fire glowed bright orange and beyond it, an empty bookcase stood against the wall.

A rustle of paper. A magazine was dropped casually onto the coffee table. 'That's the great thing about old houses isn't it,' she sighed. 'You look about and think how much you could do with it, then when it's too late, you realise how much you damn well have to.'

'Are you sorry we took the place?' he said, slipping the newspaper down next to her magazine. 'I can understand if you are. Especially stuck in here all day without proper heating.'

'Sorry!' she responded, brushing wisps of flaxen hair from her cheek, 'David, I haven't had time to be sorry. As soon as you left for the station this morning I started taking our things out of those boxes. Then I realised there wasn't anywhere to put the stuff even if I could find what I wanted. You wouldn't believe the amount of dust in the air when they were running the central heating pipes through. I daren't even use the cupboards until those men are finished.'

'I know, Chrissy, but I didn't want to risk anything going wrong with the sale. When I found out my family owned this house back in the 1880's it made the place rather special. Mind you, if we'd been able to hang on at the other house a week or two longer, believe me, I would have.'

'Oh, I suppose so,' she answered. 'I sound as if I'm blaming you but I got off to a lousy start this morning. I ruined a perfectly good cotton top on one of those damn nails we keep finding. Why people have to knock so many bloody nails into everything amazes me. Did you see that huge one sticking out above the kitchen window? Did you?'

'Yes, I looked at it this morning,' he replied. 'Is it still there?'

'No, not now. The poor man really struggled to wrench the thing out of the wall. In the end half the plaster came down with it. I won't repeat some of the language he came out with. Mind you, I can't say I blame him, and he didn't realise I was standing in the doorway. He looked so embarrassed - I had to laugh. He said he couldn't understand why previous owners had done so little with the place until now. He's right, you know. I suppose that's why it was such a bargain. Apart from being wired for electricity, I can't see much has changed since Victorian times when your ancestors lived here. Have you any idea what happened to them?'

'Not really; I gather they weren't here all that long but there must be records laying around somewhere if we ever find the time to search for them. Look, Chrissy, its six thirty. I left the office early so we could go out for dinner. What time do the workmen plan on finishing up there?'

A glance at the ceiling and she replied, 'Right now, I imagine. There's been no drilling and hammering since you arrived home - not since I took the last mugs of tea up to them, actually. They've had more tea breaks than I can remember. God knows where they put it all.'

'Same place as the dozen cans of lager I brought in for them yesterday, I expect,'

'Believe it or not, they actually stopped to play cards half way through the afternoon, you know. I walked in and -.'

142

'Cards!' he interrupted. 'The practice might be doing all right but I'm damned if I'll pay them to sit around playing cards - I -.'

A breath of cool air wafted into the room. A floorboard groaned. In the doorway leading from the hallway into the lounge stood a short, stout man in overalls that must once have been pure white but now had slipped beyond the restorative power of any detergent. Above his stubbled face was perched a white cap from under which protruded a nest of black hair. 'Sorry to butt in, guv, but we was up in the rear attic and found this.'

He held out a small plain but tarnished brass box replete with scratches and dents. Christine felt herself blush. How could he have failed to overhear their conversation?

'Oh, you found that, did you,' remarked David, rising from the chair whilst trying to sound matter-of-fact.

'Yeah, guv - up near the dormer window. It was between the joists under a bit of loose floorboard where we was runnin' the pipes.'

'Looks like an old cash box,' observed David, moving toward the man, hands pushed into his trouser pockets so as not to appear overenthusiastic about getting hold of the object. But getting hold of it was exactly what he intended. 'Can't imagine there's anything valuable in it,' he said, reaching for the box.

'God, I hope there is,' muttered Christine, peering over his shoulder.

'There is something in it guv,' said the man. 'It's locked though. Seized shut, like.'

'Oh, so you have tried to open it?' remarked Christine, disapprovingly.

David shook the box then turned it upside down. 'Mmm, yes - nothing metallic in there from the sound of it, though it's heavy enough to maybe hold something worth getting at.'

'Don't sound like it's full of gold sovereigns, then?' grinned the man.

'No, more's the pity,' said David, turning the box about.

'Well for goodness sake, David,' insisted his wife, 'open it!'

'Hmm, I don't know that I can be bothered, really. I'm sure we don't have any keys that would fit this lock.'

'David!' she glared. 'Don't be so exasperating! You know you want to see what's inside same as we do!'

'Try this, guv,' grinned the man, holding out a screwdriver.

Kneeling down with the box held hard against the floorboards, it took only moments for David to force the screwdriver blade under the edge of the metal lid. The sound of protesting metal was followed by a crack as the catch gave. David held the box away from his face as though expecting something to jump out. The lid fell back with a squeak to reveal what lay within the box.

'Well, there we are, guv!' offered the man, pushing back his cap. 'Hardly worth the effort from the looks of it.'

'It's a child's doll,' said Christine. She lifted out the small, painted wooden figure and held it beneath the light. Wide blue eyes stared from what had been an eggshell smooth, round face framed in bedraggled red hair. Red puckered lips still shone bright though its satin and lace dress was stained with age and one of the legs hung askew.

'It's broken,' she breathed. 'That's a shame – and some of the paint has flaked off her cheeks. It's quite an ugly little thing with those staring eyes, David, don't you think?'

David peered close as she propped it up on the arm of the nearest chair. 'Rather grotesque, if you ask me. I'm not sure I'd want to give a thing like that to any kid of ours, though I suppose it's no worse than some of the stuff you get on television, never mind what they look at on their computers.'

'Oh, and here's a little book,' said Christine, reaching deeper into the box.

'Right then, guv,' said the workman, picking up his screwdriver, 'me and the lads'll be off in a minute or so. We'll be back by eight thirty in the morning and should have it all connected and runnin' by end of play tomorrow. This old place will soon warm up – you'll see!'

The man departed and Christine, examining the pages of the small, red covered book said, 'David, this is a diary. There's a date in the front. It's well over a hundred years old.'

'Mmm,' he mused, peering over her shoulder at the title page, 'it must have belonged to somebody who lived in the house after my lot.'

There, in ink no longer quite black, was written large in the hand of a child, *Alice Moore, 1890.*

'God,' she breathed, fingers poised above the pages, 'I bet we're the first to see this since she hid it away, David. Isn't it absolutely fascinating? I'm going to sit down and read every word.'

'But not now, Chrissy. You'll have plenty of time tomorrow when I'm at the office. Go and get yourself ready then we can head off to the restaurant.'

***

It was past seven and dark when David arrived back from the station that following evening. He drew up by the house to find the curtains in the front lounge still open and the room brightly lit. He could see her standing by the empty fireplace, arms folded. She evidently had not heard the car nor had she seen his headlights. Curious to know what so occupied her, he stepped up to the window and tapped on the glass. She responded as though startled by an intruder. Then, with a visible sigh of relief, hurried out of the room and through the hallway to greet him as he opened the door.

'What's up?' he said, kissing her. 'You look upset.'

'Oh, it's nothing serious, darling. Well, *you* won't think so, I expect.'

'You'd better tell me anyway. Is it the central heating? Don't tell me they've cleared off without finishing the job?'

'No, the heating is on at long last. Look, I'll make some tea whilst you sort yourself out. When you come down, I'll try to explain.'

'OK, five minutes. Want to get us both a G and T instead?'

***

'So it's really bothered you?' he said, contemplating the diary where it lay innocently on the coffee table next to the glasses.

'Yes, David; I know it sounds silly but I found it quite upsetting because it all seems to have happened here in this house. Doesn't that make you think?'

'Come on Chrissy, it's just a kid's fantasy. They get it from television and the Internet nowadays. In her time they had to invent their own.'

'I dare say you're right. But it just sounds so - well, I don't know. I can't think why anyone should want to make all that up and then hide it away. Perhaps I should have looked in to see how they're managing at the shop instead of staying here all day. But with the workmen traipsing in and out, well I didn't want to -.'

'Tell you what,' he smiled, 'I'll sit and read it through after dinner whilst you watch the film. Then we'll see what I make of it.'

'I'm sorry, David, I promised I'd call around and see Julia this evening. She's only ten minutes' drive from here. Your dinner is in the oven.'

'Oh, I didn't realise you were going out. You didn't say.'

'Sorry but my mind's still full of that diary. Anyway, it will give you chance to look at it and as you say, tell me what you think. I'd feel happier if you did.'

From the open doorway he watched her car turn out of the drive and disappear into the night. Then he made his way back to the silent room and to his chair in front of the coffee table where rested the red diary. He picked it up, passed fingers over the scratched and peeling cover, looked again at the name and date before settling back to turn the pages.

The diary was not completed but remained unwritten after some two thirds of the way through the year. Many days, indeed some whole weeks, were crossed through or bore the words 'nothing today.' And though some days revealed entries of little consequence, he nevertheless determined to read the diary from its first entry, rising only to pour himself a gin and tonic.

'*January 16th*. More snow today. The Rev. Astbury came to visit Mummy this morning. Bobby is getting used to him now and wags his tail instead of barking. Bobby can stay in the room when we say prayers.

February 23rd. Very cold. Our garden pond is still frozen. I must stay away from school because I have a bad cough. Doctor Carrington says I must stay in bed all week and not get cold. I don't want to stay in bed even if it is nice and warm.

March 19th. Daddy took us to the seaside. We went by coach to the railway station and then on the train and my best friend Charlotte came too. It was cold and wet but we went to watch the fishermen working and bought some fish for our dinner. It made the carriage smell funny and people kept looking at us.'

'Hmm,' murmured David, 'must have been a decent rail service in those days.'

Scanning through the pages, he noted how careful was the handwriting, but saw where her pen had spattered blue ink onto the last week in March, then -

April 4th. A policeman came to see Mummy and Daddy. He says Aunt Rose has gone and nobody can find her and Uncle Henry is very worried. Bobby was locked away to stop him from barking until the policeman had gone.

April 5th. Uncle Henry came to see us and he is very upset. Bobby barks all the time because he dislikes Uncle Henry and Mary had to keep him in the garden.

April 8th. The policeman came to see Daddy again and I was sent out of the room. I heard them through the door talking about Aunt Rose and Uncle Henry but I do not know why because I was too far away to hear.

April 22nd. Uncle Henry came to see Daddy in the morning but I went out to go for a walk with Mary and Bobby. It was warm and sunny.

April 25th. Uncle Henry was here after lunch and I stayed in the kitchen with Mary and Bobby. I do not like Uncle Henry because he has watery eyes and a red face and bristles. Mary says he isn't my real uncle anyway. Daddy says he drinks too much but I do not know what he drinks.

May 12th. Mummy says we might buy Uncle Henry's house because it is too big for him now and Aunt Rose has gone away forever. Uncle Henry is going to live in London and that is miles away so I am glad he will not visit us so often.

June 19th. Very hot today. We have moved into Uncle Henry's house. It is bigger than our old one and has a better garden with lots of trees and more space for Bobby to play. It is not far from our old house so Charlotte and Pamela can still call to see me and Reverend Astbury too. I am glad Mary came with us even though she was asked to go and work for another family. Mary gives me sweets and I am not supposed to tell anybody.

June 22nd. I had a nasty dream in the night and woke up all cold and shivery. In my dream, someone was crying downstairs in our house. Mummy says I will have a new brother or sister before Christmas.

June 29th. I had that awful dream again and woke up frightened. It was very hot in the night and Bobby was scratching at my door. I told Mummy about my dream and she said it did not matter because it was only a dream.

June 30th. Uncle Henry came to our house today but I was at school. Mummy says he came for some business with Daddy. I am glad I was at school and he will not be coming back for weeks.

July 3rd. I was scared again last night because of the dream. I could hear the woman crying and she was still there after I awoke so I know it is not really a dream. Daddy says I am silly but I can bring the basket into my room so Bobby can sleep near my door.

July 4th. I got up last night because Bobby was growling. I let him climb onto my bed and Mary saw him in the morning. She said she would keep it secret because he is not allowed on the bed. I like Mary because she is always happy.

July 8th. Heard the woman crying downstairs again. I know Bobby can hear her too because he jumped on to my bed and his ears stood up. Mary did not hear it because I asked her in the morning and Mummy says I am dreaming but I was awake and I could see the full moon outside and long shadows from the trees on our garden.

July 11th. I heard the woman crying again last night and stayed awake for hours because it was louder. Bobby ran up and down the room and yelped but nobody heard. I do wish she would stop and go away. She is not nice. She should not be in our house.

July 12th. The Rev. Astbury was with Mummy when I came home from school but I did not tell him about the crying woman because he would say I was telling an untruth. He always says people are telling untruths if he does not agree with them. He reads to me from the Bible and he has awful breath and lots of black hairs growing out of his nose.

July 16th. I heard her crying again last night. Bobby is frightened like me and I wish Mummy and Daddy could hear her. I am too scared to go downstairs in the dark. I told Charlotte and Pamela about the woman but they think I am making it up. I am not making it up but I will not speak about it to anyone else except Mary.

July 23rd. Bobby woke me up by howling and jumping onto my bed and I heard the woman again. She was coming up the stairs so I hid under the bedclothes for ages. It was hot but I was afraid and dared not come out.'

David noted a change in the child's handwriting. It was becoming looser, less well ordered, with pre-printed dates crossed out and new ones written in to suit. All of the chatty little day-to-day entries were gone. A feeling of unease reached out from the pages to touch him like a cold hand. Central heating or no, the air in the room held a distinct chill. He was tempted to switch on the television but the little diary would not have him relinquish its tale.

July 27th. Uncle Henry is coming to see us tomorrow and mummy says I must take care of Bobby because he always barks too much.

July 28th. Something HORRID, HORRID, HORRID happened in our house today. Uncle Henry came to see Daddy after dinner and I went to the garden to play with Bobby but it rained so we came back indoors. Mummy was upstairs and Mary was busy in the kitchen so I played with Bobby in the hall. I heard the woman crying even though it was daytime and then I saw someone come up out of the cellar when the door was closed. It was dark in the hall and I thought it was Mary because she went into the drawing room where Daddy and Uncle Henry were sitting. Bobby started to crouch and bark and all his hairs stood up and he showed all his teeth. Daddy came to the door because of the noise and I ran to him. When I saw into the room there was a frightful woman standing near Uncle Henry and making a noise like cats make when they fight. She had long brown hair like Aunt Rose but she was dressed in a dirty nightgown. She was trying to scratch Uncle Henry's face and eyes with her long finger nails but her hands went right though him and Uncle Henry and Daddy took no notice of her. She kept spitting and scratching and when Uncle Henry got up she turned around. I cried because the front of her gown was all torn and red and her face and hair were covered in red too and under her face was another mouth like a big smile but all messy and red as well. Daddy came to see why I was crying and Uncle Henry came too but she followed him and made me cry even more until Mummy and Mary came and took me away. I do not know what I did then because I cannot remember and then I was in my bed with Mummy, Daddy and Doctor Carrington looking down at me.

July 29th. I have been in bed all day today and have to take medicine. Doctor Carrington called again and said it was because I have a fever and Mary has been telling me stories. Bobby is allowed to stay all the time and I have told Mary what I saw. She says it is because I am not well but says I will soon be better.

July 30th. It was very hot today and later there was thunder and lightning. After that I could still hear the woman and I am very frightened because I know she is in our house all the time and is waiting for Uncle Henry to come back. In my prayers I ask God to make her go away.

July 31st. I went to help Mary in the kitchen. Mary went down into the cellar and I started crying and tried to stop her. Mummy sent me back to my room and Mary came to see me later. She said that there was nobody in the cellar and I shouldn't worry. Reverend Astbury came to visit us after dinner and asked me what I have seen and why I cry so much. He said I should pray more often because we are all sinners and God will not help me unless I do. I do not know why I am a sinner because I have not done anything wrong and I love Mummy, Daddy, Mary and Bobby. Mummy does not like Reverend Astbury because he keeps touching her and she has to move away all the time.

August 1st. Charlotte came with her mummy today and we went to play on the swings Daddy put up in our garden under a big tree. I wanted to tell Charlotte about the crying woman but I do not think she will believe me and if I do Mary and Mummy will say it is untrue. Doctor Carrington came before dinner and took my temperature and said how pale I was and I have to take more of the nasty medicine. Daddy brought some chocolates and I shared them with Charlotte and gave three to Bobby. I can have more if I take my medicine.

August 2nd. Mummy sent me to bed early because Uncle Henry came to see Daddy and I always get upset. I hid on the landing when Mary opened the door and let him in and took his coat. When Uncle Henry went into the room with Daddy, Mary had to go to the kitchen and Bobby came up to the landing with me and started to growl. I saw the woman come up from our cellar and go along the hall and through the closed door into the room with Daddy and Uncle Henry. Bobby went to his basket in my room and I stayed to listen. I know they cannot see her because I could hear them talking but she was screaming as well so I went to my room and hid under my bed clothes to keep the sound away. Mary came upstairs with my drink and a book she is reading to me. She said she would not tell anyone I had been crying again.

August 3rd. Doctor Carrington came to see me today. He says I am still very pale and have to keep taking my medicine. He talked to Mummy for a long time then she said we would be going to the seaside. I like the seaside. I wanted to take Bobby but he cannot come with us and has to stay with

Mary. I am glad we are going away because I do not like our house anymore because that woman lives in the cellar and I am too frightened to play in the hallway. I will hide my diary in my secret box until we come home again.

August 10th. We are home. I did not want to come back because I like the seaside more than our house. I wish Daddy would take us all back to our old house. Doctor Carrington came to see me before dinner and said I looked a lot better. Bobby kept jumping up and wagging his tale.

August 11th. The woman is crying loud at night. How I hate being back here. I wish I could run away and never see our house again.

August 13th. I had the most horrid time <u>ever</u> yesterday and could not write in my diary. Daddy was taking us to see Uncle Henry and Mummy came too because she wants to see his house. I had to go because Mary was out at the shops and there was nobody to stay with me. The carriage came at eight o'clock and we all got in. We had to wait for Daddy to collect some papers and Bobby was told off for trying to jump over the gate. He started to snarl and yelp and ran away around the house. When Daddy came along the path I saw the horrible woman walking behind him. The horses began to snort and stamp their hooves and the coachman shouted at them. She was even more horrid in the sunlight because she was all torn and covered in blood and her eyes were like hot cinders. I was crying and she came nearer and got up into our coach and I tried to get out through the door away from her. She sat next to Daddy when he got in but we could not go because I was screaming and trying to get out and the man could not control our horses. She looked at me because she knows I can see her and I screamed so much they had to sit me down on the grass whilst Daddy went to Uncle Henry's on his own and said he would go to see Doctor Carrington on the way. The coach kept stopping because the horses were upset and making a lot of noise and would not walk properly. Doctor Carrington came later and said Daddy had to walk to Uncle Henry's because of the horses and he gave me some medicine to make me sleep because I was shaking so much. I did not wake up until this afternoon and Doctor Carrington was here again so I told him how unhappy I was in our house. He said Daddy knew because I had not been well since we came here and that we might have to move away. I know that when Daddy came home last night that the thing I hate so much was behind him even if I did not see it because it lives here and will never go away. I wish someone else could see it and then they would all believe me. I am frightened in case it comes into my room.

August 14th. I do not think I stayed awake very long last night. At breakfast Daddy said I was to go and stay at Charlotte's and he would sell our house before Christmas. I am very glad I am going to Charlotte's house because the horrible woman will not be there but I wish I could take Bobby as well because he is frightened of her. I will leave my diary in the little box Daddy gave me to keep things in because I never want to read it again. I will leave my doll as well because it is old and broken and looks like the woman. I will never come here again. Never. Never. Never.'

156

David closed the little book and placed it back upon the coffee table next to the empty glass. After a time deep in thought, he rose from his chair, picked the diary up and carried it over to the part-filled bookcase where rested the metal box. He placed the diary under the ragged doll and closed the lid, regretting he had damaged the box by forcing the lock rather than waiting until a key could be found. He considered how much a talking point the diary might be once they were in a position to invite guests around for dinner.

'I suppose,' he reflected, stepping over to the door, 'this is the room she imagined she saw the thing enter when old Henry came to visit. Visible from where he stood was the landing and set in the side of the wall to his right, under the rising stairs, was the door to the cellar. 'Yes, it's the only door within plain view from the landing. No wonder Chrissy was so convinced.' The air felt cold.

***

It was past eleven o'clock when he heard the front door close. When she was once more seated close by he poured drinks and asked, 'How are Julia and Nigel?'

'They're fine and they're dying to see this place when it's finished - if it ever is.'

'Oh, it will be soon. What I don't fancy is being shoved around from room to room when the decorators are in. I'd rather we weren't here at all for a week or two.'

'We could go away - down to the coast like the people in the diary.'

'I suppose we could. It's a lot easier now than it was in their day - we just get into the car. For them it must have been quite an expedition.'

'Yes, David, but people in those days weren't in such a hurry so it probably didn't matter.'

'Well, I don't know about you, but I wouldn't want to change places with them. I'd rather have the conveniences of modern life. I bet if we found ourselves without the things we take for granted now, we'd realise just how much we'd lost.'

'Perhaps,' she answered, 'but we're in so much of a rush all the time. I think we've lost a few things from their day as well.'

'We have,' he responded, 'several unpleasant diseases, a number of nasty parasites and child labour. And can you imagine living in this house with no electricity - in the depths of winter without decent heating?'

'The way it must have been when that little girl lived here and wrote her diary. You did read it, didn't you?'

'Yes I did and I stick with what I said earlier. It's got to be a hoax, or maybe she was hallucinating, though I did find something interesting.'

'A hoax – hallucinating? D'you really think so?'

'Of course I do,' he answered, gesturing dismissively with his hand, 'unless you actually believe in that kind of stuff. Someone probably concocted it and left it there, knowing it might be found later. And now it has been. By us.'

'Yes David, but - well, I'm not as convinced as you are.'

'You're just gullible,' he shrugged. 'Why *do* women take this sort of thing so seriously? Why do they get so locked into superstition, fortune telling and that sort of nonsense?'

'Bloody cheek!' she responded. 'However did you reach that conclusion?'

'Easy. When I get my evening paper at the station it's always women I see browsing through the horoscope magazines. Never men.'

'That's just harmless fun, David. Anyway who starts all the weird religious cults around the world? Not women! At least *we* didn't burn each other alive over a few disagreements. Men are the real fanatics. They go for it in a much bigger way.'

'That's different,' he replied smugly. 'They're in it for money and power. A good many of them probably don't believe a word of what they preach.'

'What a cynical old sod you are!' she responded, eyeing the now empty glasses. 'Pour me another drink. And David - what *did* you find of interest in a diary you make out is rubbish?'

'Ah, yes,' he said, reaching for the bottle, 'if there's any truth in it at all, it looks as if boozy old Henry was a direct ancestor of mine. How about that!'

'Hmm - it's a pity we don't have a photograph.'

'Maybe so but I'm pretty certain it wasn't the family who bought the place from him. We never had any ancestor called Moore, unless the name in the diary is make-believe. She might have made that up as well.'

'Yes,' reflected Christine, 'I wonder what happened to her. If she grew up and got married, her descendants might still be living in the area.

Wouldn't it be interesting if we could find out more about little Alice and her nasty uncle Henry? You might recognise a bit of him in yourself. I mean, we must all carry something of the people who went before us other than just a fondness for alcohol.'

'Oh, thanks very much, Chrissy,' he mumbled, lifting the glass. 'When I have more time, I'll check it out on one of those Internet sites.'

***

He left the house that following morning and took care not to awaken her. At three-thirty in the afternoon, at the end of an important meeting, he switched on his mobile phone and it at once informed him of attempted calls. He stabbed the keys.

'Chrissy, what's so important?'

'David, something has happened. When are you coming home?'

'What's the matter? Are you all right?'

'I'm all right, yes, but we've found something. I mean the workmen plastering the cellar have, and we've called the police.'

'God, Chrissy, what is going on?'

'David - I - there's someone at the door, it must be them now. When are you coming home?'

'Go and answer the door. I'll try and be out of here in five or ten minutes. Should catch the four o'clock if I hurry.'

***

The train journey seemed interminable and he was unable to call her. Too late he realised his mobile phone was still sitting on the office desk – overlooked in his hurry to leave. In his concern over what was happening at the house he'd omitted to grab an evening paper and being earlier than usual, knew none of the people in the carriage.

When he drove from the station car park it was raining hard and the road back to the village was congested by slow moving traffic. Turning into the drive he was confronted by a white police van parked outside the house. As he switched off the engine Christine appeared at the open front door then hurried through the rain to meet him. 'David,' she said, kissing him before he had chance to slam the car door, 'you wouldn't believe it, you really wouldn't!'

'Wouldn't believe what, for Christ's sake?' he pleaded as they hurried into the house.

'The workmen have found - oh, here's inspector Morressey.'

A figure in uniform emerged from the cellar and into the hallway. 'Ah, Mr McKenzie!'

'Yes, that's me - what is going on?'

'Your house has acquired a sudden notoriety, sir,' answered the inspector. 'You've got a murder victim on the premises. Not a recent one though - let me reassure you.'

David glanced from his wife to the inspector as the latter continued, 'Would you like to explain the situation to your husband, Mrs McKenzie or shall I?'

'No, I will. It's in the cellar David - behind the wall. The workmen found her when they were checking over the walls. Some of the stones were loose and -.'

'Found what?' he cut in. 'Found who?'

'We don't know who, sir,' offered the inspector, 'but she's been there a very long time. The lads have been photographing the remains.'

'Can I take a look?' asked David. 'You know, before you -.'

'If you really have to,' frowned the inspector, 'it is your house.' He moved aside, adding, 'If you wouldn't mind, sir, don't go too close - we don't want to disturb anything just yet.'

When he reached the bottom of the narrow stone steps, two of the men looked around. A third, busy disconnecting photographic lights from their power source, ignored the intrusion.

'I'm David McKenzie,' he offered. 'I want to look at the - the -.'

The two moved aside to observe his expression as he caught sight of the object. Of her.

An empty mantis-husk covered with grey dust, the corpse knelt within an irregular cavity scooped from the earth behind the limestone wall. What at first glance might have been mistaken for a large yellow eye, an area of bone was exposed where decayed flesh had fallen away from her cheek. Skeletal arms hung down in front of the corpse bearing what resembled the claws of a large bird. The face, its forehead resting against a protruding stone, was turned outward. Part hidden by strands of long hair - hair thick with grit and dust but recognisably a rich brown, were shrunken-purse eyelids. From hunched shoulders was draped the remains of a garment, shredded and grey but streaked and darkened at its front the colour of rust. Shrivelled lips drew back from a mouth in frozen snarl to expose long, yellowed teeth.

David moved nearer, mesmerised at the sight of that terrible face, seeing below it, across the dry-parchment flesh of the neck, a wide, grinning-mouth gash.

The voice from behind startled him. 'She's been around longer than any of us, sir. Murdered and walled up here since who knows when.'

'Since the 1880's I imagine,' muttered David.

'That remains to be seen, sir,' said the officer. 'Forensic will have fun with this one.'

Turning from the grim sight, he hurried back up the steps. Christine was in the lounge, talking to the inspector. On the coffee table stood the tin box with resting next to it, the red diary.

'I shouldn't take it too seriously, Mrs McKenzie,' said the inspector, 'it could have been written by the killer himself as some kind of weird joke. Sick minds aren't a product of this day and age no matter what people like to think.'

'When are they taking it – her, away,' asked David.

'It'll have to be in the morning now, sir, and I must insist neither of you goes down there until our team is finished.'

'God - you must be joking!' she exclaimed, 'I'm never going down there again and we're certainly not staying in this house tonight!'

'*We're* not?' queried David. 'I was thinking we might go and eat out somewhere. We don't need to come back until quite late. I'll take tomorrow off. They can manage without me.'

She regarded him with stark disbelief. 'Back here, David? No way! Not until that thing is gone. Look, I rang my mother before you got home and said we needed somewhere to sleep because of the building work. We can use her spare bedroom. I know you don't always see eye to eye with her but it's only for one evening and -.'

'Stay at your mother's!' he interrupted. 'No thanks, Chrissy, you take your car and go. I'll be better off here.'

'But David - how can you possibly spend a night in this house with - with -?'

'It's not going to be that much of a problem,' he responded. 'And at least it won't embark upon a verbal assassination of me or my family as soon as I open my mouth!'

'Well let's hope not, sir,' muttered the inspector.

***

By ten o'clock the police and Christine had gone and David was alone. He occupied himself for the next hour watching television, his sole company a large gin and tonic. Followed by another. By eleven thirty he was in bed, asleep.

***

In the still night air the church bell tolled as once it had when, long ago, a coach and pair stood before the house in a freezing dawn. In the cellar beneath the house, in the depths of cold earth, dull beetles scraped blindly in a microcosm labyrinth of hidden cavities. The stalking spider that earlier had retreated from an alien intrusion of light and sound had returned to bide its deadly time amidst grey shrouds.

In this silent well of blackness, dust streamed from the hollow to spill down the stone wall. Then a pattering of grit and small stones upon the floor.

Then the sound of unfolding, brittle parchment. To a tapping of dry sticks a sigh uncoiled through the stillness. The sigh of one who had waited through long years of oblivion for his return. The sigh of one at last freed from the chill confines of her tomb. In the blackness, two embers drifted. Very slowly, she began to ascend the steps, talon nails scratching hard stone, her voice the tortured iron grill of a forgotten sepulchre dragged open by an unseen hand. 'He has returned and I am free. He has returned and awaits me. Tonight we will be together again. Ah, yes, tonight we will embrace.'

Full length novels by this author

The Devil in Eden
The Man Who Sought Eternity
Return of The Hero
Shadow of The Beast
The Singing Stones

Further works by Jeff Clarke may be found on
www.jeffreypeterclarke.co.uk

And on his author page at:
https://fiction4all.com/ebooks/a1549.htm